A DEATH AT
A GENTLEMAN'S
CLUB

A EUPHEMIA MARTINS MYSTERY

Caroline Dunford

Published by Accent Press Ltd 2019

ISBN 9781786156488
eISBN 9781786156471

Copyright © Caroline Dunford 2019

Chapter One
An Old Friend Leaves Bertram in the Lurch

By 10 o'clock the entirety of my wardrobe lay strewn across my bedroom. I sat in my undergarments on my bed in deep despair. It appeared that during my stay of over a year at the Mullers' estate I had collected fifteen dresses, yet none of them were fit for today. I could, of course, ask Richenda if I could borrow something from her copious armoire - except I would rather die than do so.

This is not because Richenda, to whom until very recently I have been a paid companion, is an unreasonable employer. In fact, she has been quite the opposite, and we are soon to be sisters-in-law when I marry her younger brother, Bertram Stapleford. However, Richenda has less dress sense than her beloved horse, and although I have had her checked for colour-blindness, she still insists that shades such as ruby and lime can and should be seen together. Her regalia is always noticed, which she likes, but always for the wrong reasons, to which she seems utterly impervious.

There was only one thing I could think of to do. I turned to the tiny maid, a young girl from the village, who had been quietly sinking into despair and said, 'Could you please fetch Glanville?' When she left I threw myself back on my bed and gazed at the underside of the canopy above my bed. My room was one of those that had been decorated under the direction of Hans Muller, Richenda's husband, for the arrival of his new bride. Gold silk billowed about my bed and my walls were hung with a pale blue silk that, if you inspected it very closely, had the outlines of kingfishers etched upon it. The suite of furniture was carved from rosewood, and my bed was a 'troika' design, like a Russian sleigh.

In that moment I realised how spoilt I had become. I had thought nothing of these lovely surroundings. Bertram and I may be soulmates, but that doesn't change the fact that his estate on the Fens was waterlogged and crumbling. I knew he would do his best to get it into order for my arrival as his wife, but I also knew it would be unwise to get my hopes up. Bertram's income largely went on defeating the latest water incursion of his home. Really, if I didn't love him so much... but there spoke the spoilt part of me. It was not that long ago that my family had been made destitute on the death of my father, who expired in his mutton and onions, and I had entered service as a maid on the Stapleford estate. There my bedroom had been a tiny room in the attic, with an uncomfortable iron bed. There too I had been introduced to the person who would become my best friend, Merry, who currently lived on Bertram's estate with her husband Merritt. The two of them were expecting their first child, and I would be deceiving myself if I said I didn't hope to fall pregnant quickly after my marriage, so that our children could grow up together.

It is true my fiancé might not be as egalitarian as I am, but then he thinks he is marrying the daughter of a vicar, who has worked her way up from a maid in service to his family. In actual fact my grandfather is an Earl but, unfortunately, since my mother ran off with the local curate, he has let us get on with saving ourselves.

And that was yet another reason why today promised to be so trying. I was going to have to tell Bertram the truth.

There is a big difference between a baronet's son feeling he is overlooking class to marry a working girl and that same man realising that she is actually several ranks higher up the social scale than him. While I totally acquit Bertram of being concerned over my years in service - he has come a long way since I first met him - I suspect that should my heritage come out after (or even during) our wedding, he will loathe the situation. I do not mean he will loathe me, at least I hope not, but he will be wounded to the quick if he is demoted in the public eye from a knight on his white charger to the role of a vulgar social climber. It doesn't help that his elder brother, Richard, is quite rightly suspected of patricide, murder, illegally selling arms, blackmail, and kidnapping. Of course, with those kinds of credentials, the only positions open to him were as either a banker or a politician. Not being one to limit his opportunities, he took up both and now has an unhealthy influence in the corridors of power.

'You sent for me, ma'am?' Glanville said, appearing with surprising stealth at my bedside. She is a plain woman, with the arms of a washerwoman and a face that has clearly weathered harsh winters. However, she is sharp as a whip and can display a deadpan sense of humour that often passes quite over poor Richenda's head. We frequently worked together on keeping Richenda from implementing her more ridiculous schemes, although this had never been admitted aloud. I felt I could trust her - to a degree.

'I fear I have a problem, Glanville. I hope you may be able to help me.'

Glanville glanced around the room. 'The wardrobe exploded, did it, ma'am?'

I smiled. 'With my help, and that of the new

maid - Beryl, is it?'

'Beryl Tildsley, ma'am. A local girl, eager to learn. We have agreed to break with normal protocol and refer to her by her first name because Miss Amy kept referring to her as "Tiddles", like the kitchen cat.[1]

'In my opinion Miss Amy is given altogether far too much latitude,' said Glanville. 'I know the mistress was worried that she would feel displaced by the babies, but she dotes on them.'[2]

'Besides, Christmas is on the horizon,' I said. 'Did you hear what happened last year?'

'I did, ma'am, but as to your problem? I am afraid I have a list of duties to compete with the labours of Hercules to have done before luncheon.'

'Of course, Glanville,' I said feeling like a naughty schoolgirl. 'Today I am driving up to London with my fiancé to have a late luncheon with my mother, my stepfather, and my young brother. It is a while since I saw them. Bertram and I will take the opportunity to announce our engagement, and I cannot work out what on earth to wear.' I felt my eyes brim with tears and I looked quickly away. 'I'm sure it seems like a very silly problem, but I really do need your help.'

'I do not wish to presume, ma'am, but do I take it that your relationship with your mother is not exactly...?' She left the question diplomatically hanging in the air.

'I did not attend her wedding,' I said.

---

[1]Amy is the Mullers' adopted daughter. We believe she is around four or five, but the death of both her parents on the *Titanic* makes it impossible to be sure. Of Irish descent, she is as wilful as her red hair suggests.
[2]Richenda gave birth to twins some months earlier.

'Was this some time ago, ma'am? I am sure such things can be overcome. Time heals all wounds.'

'It was last month,' I said very quietly.

'Do you disapprove of your stepfather?'

'I've never met him,' I admitted.

'I see,' said Glanville. She regarded me quizzically. She knew I was not telling the whole story, but she would not push further. 'May I ask how your mother likes you to appear?'

'Ladylike,' I said.

'Modest?'

'Yes, but still elegant.'

'Style, not fashion, as it should be,' said Glanville, beginning to move among my clothing. She gathered and folded clothing as she went. 'I have observed the Mullers' seamstress is extremely talented. I would go as far as to say her clothes would pass for having been made by a decent atelier. However, we do not have the time for her to create an entire outfit.'

'I know,' I said miserably, 'but I couldn't think of what to ask for. Besides, I hate imposing on the Mullers' generosity,' I blurted out in a burst of honesty.

Glanville allowed herself to sniff loudly. This was clearly a sign of disapproval, but I wasn't entirely sure what caused the reaction. 'Your shoes, ma'am, and your gloves and hats. We should start there. And, of course, nothing bought by the mistress.'

I headed downstairs some time later only to encounter Hans in the hall. He watched me coming down the stairs with an intensity that made me blush. As I stepped off the last tread he came forward and held out his hands. Without thinking, I put my hands into his.

'My goodness, Euphemia, you look magnificent. Beautiful and elegant.'

I found I could not meet his admiring eyes and dropped my gaze. 'Glanville and the seamstress were most helpful in repurposing some of my clothes.'

Hans gripped my hands tightly. 'You did not commission a special outfit for this reconciliation with your family?' I shook my head. 'Euphemia, how many times must I tell you, this estate and its servants are at your disposal? You have done so much for this family…' His voice thickened, and he broke off. My mouth felt dry. I could not raise my head.

I will never know what either of us might have said or done next as Stone, the butler, strode into the hall with impeccable timing. Hans and I sprang apart like guilty lovers. Stone, naturally, and merely by his demeanour, made it clear that he had seen nothing suspicious. Instead, he said in his usual deep, level voice, 'Mr Bertram awaits you outside, miss. He has drawn the automobile up to the front steps.'

'Bertram is driving?'

'Indeed, miss. He is alone. There is no sign of McLeod.'

I turned to Hans. 'I fear something is wrong. I must go to him.'

Hans nodded. 'Of course.' His colour was a shade higher than normal, but otherwise he was his normal, suave self. 'If there is anything you need, you know you only have to let me know.'

I felt heat flooding into my face again.

'Sister,' added Hans, I assumed for form's sake. Hans and I will become brother and sister-in-law, so soon we will all be one family. A happy one, I hope.

6

'Hopefully, it is no more than McLeod coming down with a bad cold,' I said. 'You know how Bertram must be careful of his health.'

'Indeed, his weak heart is a worry to us all,' said Hans. His response sounded more automatic and emotionless than I would have liked. I gave him a swift smile and went to pick up my small case.

'Stone will take it,' said Hans before I had the chance to lift it. 'A lady never carries her own luggage. At least, not in my house.'

I smiled again. Stone picked up the case and I followed him quickly outside.

Bertram was leaning against his vehicle, smoking - a practice I cannot abide, unless it is a health-promoting cigar. At the sight of me he threw his cheroot to the ground and opened his arms wide to embrace me. Stone disappeared around the back of the automobile to busy himself loading my luggage. Bertram enveloped me in a bear hug, which quickly morphed into a passionate kiss. Although I felt my reputation must now be in tatters with the staff, I did not protest. Indeed, I have always found kissing Bertram the most uplifting experience. We broke apart when both of us ran out of breath.

'I think we embarrassed old Stone. He didn't even stop to say hello. I even remembered to carry some loose change to tip with,' said Bertram.

'Where is Rory?' I asked. 'Wasn't he meant to drive?'[3]

Bertram released me and slumped back against the vehicle. 'Ah. Bad business, that.'

---

[3]When I was a maid I was once engaged to Rory McLeod. I have never told either man this, but Bertram kisses much better than Rory does.

My hand flew to my mouth. 'He hasn't...?' I couldn't bring myself to say the word.

'Yes,' said Bertram. 'He's left me. Very bad show.'

'Good Lord,' I said. 'I thought you meant he was dead!'

'Might as well be,' said Bertram. 'Said the new situation was too much for him and he needed to start over.'

'Did he mean... me?' I faltered.

'Yes, it appears my marrying the help has offended his delicate sensibilities.' Bertram gave me a level look, daring me to suggest it was anything else, like jealousy.

'Indeed,' I quickly agreed. 'He has always been very proper about how the different classes should interrelate. But he has been your major-domo for so long. I thought, after everything, you were close - or as close as a man and his valet can be.'

Bertram nodded solemnly. 'Indeed, it is a deep and trusting relationship. His desertion has cut me to the quick, Euphemia. Why, I even had to pack my own suitcase - and you know how inept I am at that!'

'Maybe he will come back,' I suggested. 'He may only need time to accustom himself to the situation.'

'Doubt he'll have the choice,' said Bertram as he opened the vehicle door for me. 'He asked Fitzroy for a situation.'[4]

I sank down into the seat. 'I wasn't aware that Fitzroy had a particular interest in Rory's career.'

'You probably know more than I do about the way that

---

[4]Fitzroy is the enigmatic spy who has tricked, tasked, and ordered us into various adventures for the sake of King and Country.

wretched man thinks,' said Bertram. 'You've worked with him the most.' He walked round to the other side and climbed in.

'Not by choice,' I said hotly.

Bertram put his hand on my knee. 'I know that, my love. Let us hope that if nothing else comes out of this sorry state of affairs, Fitzroy uses McLeod from now on and leaves us alone.'

I smiled widely. 'If I never had to hear Fitzroy's name again I would be more than content.'

'Jolly good,' said Bertram. 'Time to leave. I can't say I'm not nervous, but meeting your family today will bring us that next step closer to marriage - and I am looking forward to that.' He returned my smile so warmly I glowed with the expectation of being kissed again. But before he could move towards me the whole vehicle shook.

'Oh, the lovebirds,' said Richenda from the back seat. 'That feeling, it doesn't last, you know.'

'What the hell are you doing in my motor?' roared Bertram.

'Why, coming to London with you,' said Richenda sweetly. 'I've already put my things in the boot.'

'Well, you bloody well can't!' said Bertram.

'Just watch me,' said Richenda.

Chapter Two
Bertram and Richenda Make a Very Bad Impression on a Member of the Clergy

'This bickering is worse than anything Amy and her peers might cause!' I cried.

'I am not getting out,' said Richenda. 'And that is final.'

'I am damn well not taking you,' said Bertram. 'Therefore, we will sit here, and I will miss my introduction to my in-laws. This will, in turn, cause the wedding to be abandoned and for Euphemia to remain a lonesome spinster for the rest of her miserable life.' He turned round to glare at his sister. 'Is that what you want? Is it?'

'Bertram!' I gasped.

'Don't be stupid, Bertram. She is a beautiful woman. Even my husband would have married her, if she had money. She'll find someone else. Probably someone taller.'

I had been going to thank Richenda for her affirmation that I wasn't entirely loathsome to the male population, but I saw my poor Bertram cringe. He hated being short.

'Or maybe that Fitzroy character I met at the hotel. He seemed most presentable.'

'Fitzroy!' I echoed in horror.

'She would never…' uttered Bertram in a voice that lacked the conviction I would have expected to hear.

'No, never,' I said. 'Now, be sensible, both of you. I would not put off the wedding, but it would be very rude to arrive late for luncheon with my mother, not to mention my new stepfather.'

'Almost as rude as missing their wedding?' said Richenda.

I ignored the comment. 'Why do you want to come to town, Richenda? I do not believe my stepfather will have included you in his plans, although he would not be impolite enough to turn you away - at least, I assume so, as he is a bishop.'

'And must have to deal with rude, ignorant, self-absorbed idiots every day,' said Bertram, who had a poor view of most congregations.

'It won't be any fun, Richenda,' I said bluntly. 'You'll be bored, and the food isn't liable to be up to much either.'

'I don't know…' began Bertram, but I kicked him hard in the foot.[5]

'I can't stay here,' said Richenda, sulkily.

'Why?' I asked. I sighed. 'Have you had another row with Hans?'

'I saw you saying goodbye to him.' She pouted. 'I merely commented on what I observed.'

'Euphemia?' said Bertram.

'He took my hands when he said goodbye,' I said. 'That is all. He didn't even give me a brotherly peck on the cheek.'

'He held them for ages,' said Richenda. 'He never holds my hand.' Her voice broke. Bertram and I glanced at one another in fright. A sobbing Richenda was the last

---

[5]Not an easy feat to do to a driver from the passenger seat, but I have a long history of striking Bertram below the knee to quiet him. I am considering buying him steel-toed boots, and an olive branch, as a combined wedding gift.

thing we needed.

'I could try and lift her out,' said Bertram quietly to me.

'Try it,' said Richenda, in a suddenly solid voice.

'No,' I said. 'It would be inappropriate. Not to mention bad for your heart. She will have to come with us. If we do not leave now we stand no chance of getting there on time.'

'Bother,' said Bertram. He pulled a fierce face and pulled down his driving goggles with a determination that alarmed me.

'Why isn't McLeod driving? Where is he?' asked Richenda. But any answer I might have given was lost in the scattering of gravel as Bertram fish-tailed his 'motor' in a speedy take-off. Richenda and I, as one, grabbed our hats. The wind took my breath quite away as Bertram swung the wheel the other way to straighten the vehicle, then roared down the drive. As far as I was concerned there would be no more time for conversation. I would be too busy praying that we survived my fiancé's driving.

We pulled up outside my stepfather's club with no more injury to us than a pair of wind-battered hats and dishevelled locks. The Holby Club could not have been more unlike Bosenby's, where I had had such an unfortunate experience. It was a large, white-fronted terraced house that could have been the townhouse of a rich family. In reality it was three houses interlinked and extended. From the outside it was elevated slightly from the road by a few blazingly white steps that made it appear a little superior and aloof. Rather, I suspected, like its members.

Richenda and I stumbled our way out of the vehicle and regarded one another.

'You look like your horse tossed you in a hedge, I'm afraid,' I said to Richenda.

To my surprise she grinned. 'You look like one of Amy's drawings,' she said.

I shivered. 'That bad?' Amy had a habit of drawing stick figures and then scrawling crazy spirals on the tops of their heads. 'We need to visit the powder room.'

Bertram had got out and was at the front of his motor car, patting the bonnet and telling it it was a good girl. He glanced over at me to smile and it took all my self-control not to burst out laughing. Richenda had no such qualms.

'You look like a hedgehog!' she roared. A well-dressed gentleman climbing the steps behind us turned to examine her through his monocle with a heavy frown. Richenda and I had worn veils over our faces and thus kept our complexions clean. Bertram had only worn goggles, so along with his wild hair, which stuck out in stiff, pomaded curls, his face was blackened with dirt, except where his driving goggles had been.

Bertram looked down at his reflection in the bonnet of the motor. 'Ye gods!' He exclaimed. 'I do!'

'We cannot allow my mother to see us like this,' I said.

'Indeed not,' said Bertram.

Richenda leaned over and examined herself in the shiny metal. 'I think it's rather funny. It's not as if we weren't spruced up before the trip. Bertram went too fast. That is all.'

'I would rather my mother's first impression of Bertram was not to think of him and his family as a laughing stock,' I said acidly.

Richenda shrugged. 'Then we had better find somewhere we can clean up inside.' She moved away and began to climb the steps.

Bertram gave me a startled look and then bolted after her. I followed more slowly. I had no wish to see Richenda trying to storm the male bastion of a Gentlemen's Club. I thought it quite likely she would fail to mention to the porter that we were invited, and would enjoy an indulgent, and pointless, argument with him about why she could not be admitted. I did not envy Bertram the trouble of sorting this out, but neither did I feel inspired to step into the fray. My nerves, usually resolute and compliant, felt shredded and sore. Bertram's driving had been breath-taking, in the worst of ways. Ever since the moment he told me that Rory had moved on, the day seemed to have gone from bad to worse. I wondered if I could pay someone to shut Richenda in a small room until we had finished our meal. If they sent in cake, then perhaps she would not mind too much. In fact, if the cake was good enough – or rather large enough, she might not mind at all.

I mounted the final step and gave my hat a half-hearted tug to straighten it. I felt a coil of hair unroll down my back as I did so. I could have wept, but I lifted my chin and marched forward. A straight-faced doorman opened the large oak-panelled door for me.

The inner chamber was painted white and lit by sunny skylights in such a way that the day could peer in upon the occupants, but the outside world was firmly shut out. The lobby held a front desk with pigeonholes behind it; around the edges of the chamber were dotted a few small standing desks where members could dash off a note or a telegram and pass it to the porter. It was a sparsely furnished room but contained a few tall pot plants to give those writing some privacy. No doubt it was normally a haven of tranquility, but not today.

At the front desk, all speaking at once, were Bertram,

still in his hedgehog guise, Richenda, gesturing wildly and making herself look even more like a creature out of its wits, and a very tall, thin man in a smart grey suit who had a bass voice. This broke over the others.

'All I am saying is, these people do not have the appearance of the guests I am awaiting. It is possible this gentleman is who he claims to be, but this lady is certainly not the one I am expecting.' He produced a monocle from his pocket and examined Richenda. 'Is there a doctor in the house? I fear she is quite hysterical.'

'I am not hysterical,' shouted Richenda, 'I am a suffragette and I demand entrance as an equal human being of status!'

Bertram was umming and erring and trying to get a few words in without appearing uncivil enough to actually interrupt. He was definitely the one losing in the three-way conversation.

It was at this stage I managed to glimpse the head of a man, shorter than Bertram, wearing a plain, dark grey waistcoat and tie. Looking to be in his early thirties, it was clear from his furrowed brow, and way he kept scratching at his balding pate, that he couldn't get the situation under control.

I took a deep breath and then, in an accent my mother had so carefully polished to diamond sharpness, and which I did my best to keep hidden as both a servant and a fiancée, I said in a stern, projected voice, 'My goodness, what on earth is going on here? I had been led to believe this was a gentlemen's establishment, but I fear I have entered the wrong building.'

As short, sharp sentences go, it wasn't. But my accent, the verisimilitude of how a Earl's daughter spoke, caused a complete silence to fall before I finished speaking.

The little man from behind the desk, perhaps sensing help despite my tumbled appearance, asked, 'And you are, ma'am?'

'The Honourable Euphemia Martins. I am here to dine with my mother and my new stepfather, The Bishop. The journey has been trying and I would appreciate the opportunity to powder my nose before joining my family. I have come some distance.'

'Of course, ma'am,' said the little man. I believe if he had had a forelock he would have tugged it. As it was, he merely gave a little dipping bow. 'I shall summon a page to direct you immediately.' Richenda stood looking at me with her mouth wide open. Bertram had gone an unfortunate shade of red. The tall thin gentleman, however, came forward and kissed me on the cheek. It was only then I saw the cross around his neck.

'I would know Philomena's daughter anywhere,' he said and smiled in a most avuncular manner.

'Oh, good heavens,' I said, 'are you my mother's bishop? I mean...?'

The smile deepened, and I saw a twinkle in his eye. 'I know exactly what you mean. Despite being dedicated to God, and having a congregation, I am most certainly your mother's bishop. May I say how delighted I am to meet my new stepdaughter.'

My hand flew to my hair. 'An open-topped motor vehicle, I imagine,' said The Bishop. 'Ah, to be young again. I do not believe the Archbishop would condone me driving one, but I feel they must be rather fun, are they not?'

'It was a startling drive,' I said. 'Breath-taking in places. We were a little late in departing.'

'Ah, I see. I assume you were not doing the actual

16

driving yourself?'

'No,' I said.

The Bishop muttered something under his breath that, for a moment, I thought was 'Pity', but I was distracted by the arrival of the page.

'If you would follow me, ma'am. I'll take you to the ladies' facilities.'

I exited with him quickly, not caring whether Richenda followed or not. I only wanted to get away.

The page led us to a door that opened into a very well-appointed powder room attached to the necessary utilities. I took off my hat at once and began brushing out my hair. After that I thoroughly washed my face and hands before putting my hair back up and my now-straightened hat back on. I took off my jacket and shoes. I would need to get the page to brush and polish these.

'Are you taking off all of your clothes?' asked Richenda. 'Only, you being of the old nobility, I don't know what you might be capable of.'

I froze. Then I turned to face the storm. Richenda met my eye and began to laugh. Softly at first, but gradually she broke into a huge belly laugh. In a few moments I could not help joining her.

'Oh, my goodness, Euphemia, what will you do next? I never thought for one moment they would believe your silly voice, but you kept the charade going wonderfully. Honourable indeed. I'll say something for this bishop your mother has married, he's a jolly good sport.'

This was the moment to tell her that neither my demeanour nor my title had been fake. I took a deep breath. But before I could speak Richenda said, 'Actually, that's a good idea. I wonder if that page could do anything with my hat. I think some of these decorative birds are positively bald now. Really, Bertram's driving is too much.' She scooped up my shoes and jacket and flounced through the door. Fortunately, the page, who must have been warned that we needed to be contained, was waiting outside and took these, as well as Richenda's shoes. She returned and slumped down in one of the chintz armchairs that had been provided for recovering ladies. I fled back to the washbasin and finished tidying up as much as I could.

By the time I had finished and helped Richenda redo her hair - her efforts were quite hopeless - the page had knocked on the powder room door and returned our items. I surveyed myself in front of the long mirror. I expected some remarks from my mother, but overall I had scrubbed up a lot better than I had hoped. The clothing that Hans' seamstress and Glanville had altered fitted me handsomely. Richenda's appearance remained raggedy, but she seemed unaware, so I let it go.

I opened the door and considered how to make a polite request that Richenda made herself scarce.

'I've been thinking,' said Richenda suddenly, 'I know it was a bit much for me to foist myself on you, but now The Bishop has seen me, perhaps I could come and say hello. I will not even take a seat. If they have never met Bertram before you won't want me hanging around.'

'Thank you,' I said.

'If I wasn't so ferociously angry with Hans, I would never have come,' said Richenda with a sorrowful sniff. Richenda weeping was the last thing we needed.

'I will speak to him,' I said. 'Everything will be fine.'

Richenda gave me a watery smile. 'You've always been far nicer than me,' she said. I dodged the hug she was about to give me by darting through the doorway. I feared she would knock my hat off again, for she was not a lady known for her agility, except on horseback.

I caught the little page kicking his heels against the skirting board. He straightened up the moment he saw me. 'Ma'am, can I take you through to your party? Ma'ams,' he added as Richenda barged through the door behind me.

'Thank you, that would be most helpful. Can you tell me if the gentleman who was with us has already joined them?'

'No, ma'am. But he left this note for you.' He pulled a folded paper from his pocket and handed it to me.

Surprisingly, it was un-crumpled, but then the paper was of excellent quality. I opened it to see the club's emblem and address at the top. Below it I recognised Bertram's scrawl.

My Love,

I am mortified that your stepfather's first impression of me was that of me looking like prospective wildlife. I intend to take my time restoring my appearance and, if you will forgive me, enjoying a restorative brandy - for my heart, naturally.

It has also occurred to me that it might be easier for you to break the news that you are marrying into the minor nobility alone. I appreciate a prank as much as the next man, but I could see from The Bishop's face that he was quite taken aback at your boldness, suggesting you were of the upper ranks. Having married your mother, he can be in no doubt as to your true status. Of course, this carries no weight with me, but the Church is a hierarchical institution and he may have thought the joke improper. If I step in and introduce myself as the son of a Baronet, he may feel we are marrying out of the natural order. Therefore, I think it is better if you assail his defences first and explain your prank was well-intentioned. He will see that you are not attempting to put yourself above your class, so that when I join you later for Luncheon, he will not, with luck, be in the mood to object to our nuptials.

With undying Love
Your Bertram

'The pig!' I cried.

Richenda, who had had no qualms in reading over my shoulder said, 'He probably does need a bit of a rest after all the driving and the later fuss. He does have a dicky heart. But yes, I hate to say it about my brother, but he does come over as a bit of a faint-heart.'

'Craven coward!' I said. 'And his personal comments directed at me!'

'Well, he is a man,' said Richenda. 'In the end they all try to patronise one and control one. Even the best of them. I should know.' She patted me on the arm. 'Never mind, Euphemia. I have more moral fibre than the rest of my family put together. I shall escort you.'

At that moment I was too upset with Bertram, and too caught up with my own predicament, to think of anything other than feeling grateful to her. The little page led us back through to the club's main lobby and then took us into the coffee lounge. It was laid out with lots of tables across the main stretch of the room, but there were also seated areas spaced out around the periphery for those who required a little more privacy. Today, all the tables sported bright white cloths and tiny crystal vases of white, purple, and pink flowers. This, I imagined, was part of the effort for Ladies' Day. However, the room was surprisingly empty. The coffee lounge might easily have contained fifty or sixty guests, but I noted, in estimation, that it was currently less than twenty per cent full. Other than my mother and Richenda, I saw only two other ladies. Clearly, this new-fangled habit of letting ladies in to the club was not going down well.

The page took us over to an excellently situated table under a window. As we approached I saw a lanky, boyish figure with his back to us, swinging on the back legs of his chair. 'Joe!' I cried out before I could stop myself. The boy turned. His face was longer than I recalled, but it was clearly my little brother.

'Effie!' he cried out even more loudly and, pushing back his chair, raced across the room to embrace me. He hit me with the full force of a twelve-year-old and winded me. I was glad I had suppressed the urge to pick him up and whirl him in the air as I had done when we were both younger. I returned his embrace, hugging him tightly.

'Good heavens,' I managed to say, 'you're almost up to my shoulder.'

Joe looked up at me, his chin resting against my chest with his brown eyes twinkling. 'I'm going to be tall like our Step-pa,' he said. 'Really, really tall. Oh Effie, it is so topping to see you again. Did Mother tell you? I'm a chorister now! I go to the cathedral school and have to sing so loudly. But I don't have to board because we live right next door! And Step-pa is going to take me around the labyrinth tomorrow. But he says there isn't a Minotaur. Do you think it could be because they haven't looked properly yet? You could come and help, Effie. If anyone could find a monster, it would be you!'

'Joe, release your sister at once and return to your seat!' My mother's familiar tones rang out - not loudly of course, that would be ill-bred, but with the clear-cut intonation of a lady raised in an Earldom.

21

Richenda had moved ahead to the table because she had heard my mother's voice. 'Mrs Martins! What are you doing here?' In that moment I flashed back to when my mother had arrived unannounced at the Muller estate. She had been staying with a local vicar and his family and had heard talk of the new companion Mrs Muller had employed. By some means known only to her she had figured out that it might be me.

At the time Richenda had been delighted to introduce me to her new friend, the Earl's daughter. For whatever reason, once my mother had confirmed I was well, appeared happy and was now a companion, rather than a maid, she had seen fit to not undermine my ruse. But, as they say, the truth will out.

'Ah,' I said, still clinging onto the not-so-little Joe. 'I think we are about to have a problem.'

'Is that the one you wrote looks like her horse and has the dress sense of a drunken baboon?' said Joe in a distressingly loud stage whisper.

Fortunately, Richenda did not appear to hear. She was too busy chatting to my mother. While she was doing this, I had a chance to whisper urgently to Joe that the tales I had written to him were meant for his ears only and they were all made up anyway. Joe gave me a conspiratorial wink but stopped talking. I walked across with my arm around my little brother's shoulders.

'Richenda,' I said interrupting her. 'I must beg your forgiveness. You see, Mrs Martins is my mother. She did not disclose this when you first met her. It is entirely my fault. I had placed her in a very difficult position. She had been trying to find me for some time. She thought it was possible I was working as a servant at your estate, but she didn't know. I am sure the only reason she did not give me

22

away was not to embarrass you at the time.'

Richenda turned on me, a look of confusion on her face. 'What do you mean? Is what your mother says true? You are the grand-daughter of an Earl?'

'Quite so,' said The Bishop, who had risen at Richenda's approach and looked even taller now (if such a thing were possible). 'Perhaps we should all sit down and have a nice cup of tea.'

I was expecting Richenda to explode with indignation. I couldn't in my wildest dreams have imagined what she would do next, and it took me quite by surprise.

She laughed.

Not wildly with hysteria. Instead she gave a deep, genuine chuckle. 'I always knew there was more to you than at face value,' she said to me. 'An Earl's granddaughter, no less. No wonder you were so annoyed by Bertram's note. Oh, his face...' She laughed again and had to hold on to the back of an empty chair to steady herself before continuing. 'His face when he realises he's the one marrying up in the world. Oh, goodness, it's been worth enduring his driving to learn this. He is going to be so, so, so utterly overcome!'

'I fear so,' I said quietly. 'Richenda, it must seem as if I have played the most horrible trick on you all...'

Richenda placed a hand on my arm. 'If anyone knows how disagreements can shatter families, it is I. My father and I - well, we never reconciled before he died.' She paused a moment as an expression of sadness overcame her. Then she turned to my mother. 'While I am unaware of the circumstances, not that it is any of my business, why you and Euphemia parted, that you came looking for her suggests you still feel that you are bound together. May I say that during her time with my family, Euphemia has

23

shown herself to be intelligent, compassionate, and more loyal than my own kin. She is a first-rate woman and I am not at all surprised that she is so closely related to an Earl. But, regardless of her station, I count it an honour to be her friend. I hope she will still marry into my family, for then I will have the privilege of calling her sister, something I very much hope to do.' Then she stepped forward and kissed me on the cheek. 'Good luck,' she whispered and walked away from the party with a quick, decisive tread.

'She seems very nice,' said Joe loudly.

'She is,' I said, swallowing back a tear. 'In a pinch, she always comes up to scratch.'

'Well,' said my mother. 'As far as your employer is concerned, I am the villain in the piece.'

'Villainess, my love,' said The Bishop, holding out a chair for me. 'Please do join us, Euphemia. I imagine your mother and you have much to discuss. And Joe, one too many interruptions from you, young man, and I will send you out to wait in the motor car.'

'And miss luncheon!' said Joe in horror.

'*And* miss being with your sister,' said The Bishop.

'Oh, that too,' said Joe. 'Sorry, Effie.' He sat down beside me and clamped his lips together so tightly, it was hard not to laugh.

Chapter Three
Euphemia Reveals All and Bertram is Furious

'Perhaps we should start with how your employer, and her brother - it is her brother you are intending to marry, is it not?' said The Bishop.

I nodded.

'How her brother, your fiancé, does not know of your real station in life?'

'Well, the thing is…' I said, 'the first time he met me I was working as a maid at his father's house. And then there was the matter of the dead body.'

The Bishop raised an eyebrow, looking for all the world like a slightly bemused but tolerant eagle.

'Euphemia, we don't need to go into any of that with your stepfather,' said my mother. 'Now, who is this man you are intending on marrying? I thought you had a particular aversion to marriage, seeing as you could not bring yourself to attend your own mother's wedding.'

'It was grand,' said Joe beside me. 'I gave Mother away, and afterwards there was the most excellent feeding.'

'Really, Husband,' said my mother. 'My son does say the most ridiculous things. He claims he picks them up from the boys at school. Are you certain it is a proper place?'

'It has been thought so for the past six hundred years,' said The Bishop gently. 'The truth is, Euphemia, I would dearly like to hear about all your adventures, but I don't believe we have even been properly introduced yet.'

'Joe,' hissed my mother.

Joe stood up. 'Sister, may I present your new Step-pa, my Lord Bishop of -, the Right Reverend Giles Hawthorn. My Lord, your new stepdaughter, Euphemia. The family calls her Effie.'

'We most certainly do not,' said my mother.

The Bishop formally took my hand. 'It is a pleasure to meet you, Euphemia. Are you comfortable calling me Step-pa as Joe does? I am sure there are other nomenclatures we could use. Even Giles, if you wish. I will understand if you do not wish to address another as Father.' He smiled at me with extraordinary kindness.

Many thoughts went through my head as I looked up at him. That my mother had at last married her Lord. Even if he was a Lord of the Church and not of state. That he was both completely like my father and unlike him. I recognised the same compassion in The Bishop that my father had always shown the world, but where my father was a man beaten down by life, struggling on as best he might, here was a strong man, at the height of his career, assured not only of his place in the Church but recognised by it as a man of use. I felt a twinge at the thought. If my father had not been a country vicar, with no hope of advancement after his shocking marriage, perhaps he too might have risen in the clergy. But that was not The Bishop's fault. I also recognised him as a man shrewd enough to appreciate my mother's intelligence, but also her pain at being cast out from her own world. He would doubtless treat her with all kindness, but he would not allow unkindness or unthinking hurt to occur on his watch. I thought him just the man for whom my mother was now. If only he could survive Joe's disappointment upon finding that there was really was no Minotaur in the labyrinth, I thought he would do rather well in our family.

'Euphemia, answer your stepfather!' hissed my mother.

I blushed. 'I am so sorry. I would be most happy to call you Step-pa as Joe does.'

'Excellent,' said The Bishop. 'Now, I would love to hear all about your adventures, but I believe we have your young gentleman to meet. Does he really not know about your background?'

'I was going to tell him on the way here,' I said. 'But, unfortunately, his major-domo gave notice recently, so he was driving us himself. I didn't want to distract him,' I said. Nor, I thought, did I have the breath to spare.

'But you accepted his proposal without him knowing who you are?' interjected my mother.

'Rather like Cinderella, don't you think, my dear?' said The Bishop. 'I think you said he is the son of a Baronet. He is obviously not marrying her for her station. Not that I personally believe such a thing is so important. It is much more a meeting of minds that counts in a marriage. I believe a couple must suit one another. It is rare that this happens across the classes, due to upbringing, education, et cetera, but when it does I think the class difference becomes the least important aspect of the union.'

My mother gave The Bishop a look that spoke volumes.

'Ah, Euphemia, it would seem your mother wishes to remind me that I am not currently in the pulpit.'

My mother gasped slightly. The Bishop took her hand and gave it a little squeeze. My mother's colour rose, and she removed it gently, but she didn't seem too unhappy about this display of matrimonial affection.

'I suppose it might mean he genuinely loves you,' she said.

'I expect him to be mortified when he knows the truth,' I said. 'He is very aware of station.'

'Quite right too,' said my mother.

'Ah, you miss the problem, my dear. The young man in question believes Euphemia to come of good moral stock - a vicar's daughter. Your mother said you had told him that much?' I nodded. The Bishop continued. 'But, as it stands, he believes he is the knight sweeping in to bear off the village maiden into matrimony rather than it being somewhat the other way around.'

'It is not as if I am an heiress,' I said. 'I'm merely an Honourable.'

'Of course you are,' snapped my mother. 'Your grandfather might have cut me out of his will, but he didn't do so to either you or Joe.'

For the first time in my life I felt my jaw physically drop. 'Er… how much?' I managed to gasp.

My mother named a far from insignificant sum.

'Oh no,' I said. 'He will never marry me now.'

'Pride is a terrible sin,' said The Bishop. At this point we all turned and looked at the poor man. He held up his hands, silencing himself.

'It is not insurmountable,' said my mother. 'The money can always be entailed upon your children. But where will you live? At the Palace with us? As a spinster daughter that might have been possible, but I do not think as a married couple the Deanery would be happy.'

'He has an estate,' I said. 'In the Fens. It is comprised of some farms and cottages as well as a larger house and stables. It is not a Great House, but it is respectable. It is called White Orchards.'

'Never heard of it,' said my mother. 'Good Heavens. In the Fens!'

'Mother, you know even if it had been possible, I would never have wanted to run a Great House. I have too many other interests I wish to follow.'

My mother dabbed her eyes with a handkerchief. 'That was your father's fault, God rest his soul. A good man but with the strangest ideas about educating daughters. Intelligence is about as much use to an unmarried girl as having a pair of hooves.'

'I believe,' said The Bishop, 'that intelligence is a gift from God and should not be squandered.' At this point I noticed Joe had been slyly drawing on the table cloth with a pencil. He had tallies under M, S-P and E. I realised he was attempting to keep score.

'But you would not actively set up a school for girls, would you, Bishop?' said my mother.

'I have never really thought about it, I am ashamed to say,' answered The Bishop. 'Perhaps I should.'

My mother looked horrified at falling into her own trap. Joe marked another one up under S-P.

'My main problem with all this,' said The Bishop, 'is that we are due to have luncheon. And I know Joe will side with me in agreeing that that is important.'

'Very important,' said Joe.

The Bishop nodded at him. 'I think there are a few things here that might affect the digestion. Might I suggest you go and fetch your young man, Euphemia, and we get everything out in the open. We can discuss where we go next over our meal. Breaking bread together is always a most communal moment. It will inspire us to find solutions fitting to all.'

'It will also stop my stomach rumbling,' said my single-minded brother.

I was rising to my feet when a discreet waiter, who

seemed to appear from nowhere, approached our table. He had placed his hands deferentially behind his back, and his aged forehead was deeply frowned. He bowed very slightly to The Bishop. 'My Lord, I am very sorry, but I fear we may not be able to accommodate you and your party for luncheon today. I extend our deepest apologies.'

I froze, half risen. My life has been full of calamities and sudden disasters. Could it be that this disastrous trail had followed me into the refined air of a respectable Gentlemen's Club?[6]

'Sit down, Euphemia,' hissed my mother. 'You look most odd.' I slumped back down into my seat. Not everything, I told myself, is associated with murder or Richard Stapleford. Perhaps something of a minor inconvenience had occurred, such as the kitchen catching fire.

'Indeed,' said The Bishop, 'that is most inconvenient.' Joe had the sense to keep his mouth shut, but his eyes were wide, and he was nodding visibly.

'What a great shame,' I said. 'We shall have to reconvene another time.'

'How convenient for you.' said my mother. 'I assume something of a similar sort occurred when you were unable to attend my wedding.' She gave me a look that could have curdled vinegar.

'I am afraid, my Lord, the matter is quite out of my control. Indeed, if anything, it might be said to be more in your remit than mine!'

I felt my heart drop into my boots. 'Has someone

---

[6]The *other* Gentlemen's Clubs I have encountered are ones that I sincerely hope my new Step-pa has no notion of existing.

died?' I said.

'Euphemia!' exclaimed my mother. 'That is a highly illogical and inappropriate question.'

I felt like retorting that it was highly inappropriate for one's mother to criticise one in front of the staff, but I suspected that when she was a girl and lived in the Earl's Great House, she had belonged to the set that regarded servants as little more than furniture. Whimsically, I wondered if, as a maid, she would have regarded me as equal to a footstool or having the status of a small, but uncomfortable chair.[7] The waiter gave me a sharp look. 'The young lady is most acute.'

I sighed. Fortunately, this was overshadowed by my mother's dramatic intake of breath. Joe's eyes positively bulged from his head. Knowing him, I did not take this as a sign of fear, but of intense curiosity. However, The Bishop put his hand on Joe's shoulder. 'I suppose you do have a number of elderly members,' he said. 'Nature will take its course. God calls those when he chooses, not when we desire. There are worse places to leave this earth than among one's comrades and old friends. Would you like to me say a prayer over the deceased?'

'That would be most kind, sir,' said the waiter, 'and most reassuring to the staff. You'll understand we feel we must close the restaurant out of respect?'

'Oh, quite, quite,' said The Bishop. Joe adopted a mulish expression but continued to keep his tongue between his teeth. He had grown up a lot since I had last seen him. 'If you wouldn't mind waiting, my dear?' The Bishop said to my mother. 'And if you, sir, could ask the

---

[7] I had the sense not to enquire.

porter at the front desk to make enquiries about local restaurants where one might still be able to procure a meal of a reasonable nature? We are a party of five. Or is it six, counting the other Lady you had with you, Euphemia?'

'Yes, where are they?' asked my mother. 'I should like to leave as soon as possible.' She lowered her voice. 'Before Joe gets any ideas,' she said softly to The Bishop. 'I don't want him having nightmares.'

'No, indeed,' said The Bishop. 'If I might also trouble you, my good man, to collect the other members of our party.'

'Mrs Hans Muller,' I supplied, 'And Mr Bertram Stapleford.'

The little waiter nodded, the frowns deepening on his face as he mentally tucked away his tasks. At this rate he would end up with a face like a walnut.

'I'm sure everything will be quite all right,' I said. 'Unless, of course, there is any reason to be concerned over the poor gentleman's demise.'

'Like plague,' said Joe eagerly.

'Nothing. Nothing at all,' said the waiter.

The quickness and sharpness of his return gave me pause. 'There is nothing questionable about this death?' I asked and my voice, from years of working alongside the wretched Fitzroy, must have sounded quite stern and professional as the poor man broke down into tears.

The faces of everyone else at the table went into frozen astonishment. The Bishop's class of people, and the ones my mother continued to count herself a member of, do not cry in public. Joe had doubtless never seen a man cry before. My experience was wider. I stood up and took the waiter by the shoulder, steering him to an empty table that was shielded from the rest of the room by fashionable potted foliage. The Bishop followed me, rather like a sheep that has suddenly found itself on an unknown path and opts to follow the person looking most like a shepherd. I attracted the attention of a different waiter and commanded him to bring water and brandy.

'If you say so, miss,' said the second waiter. 'But whose bill should I put it on? We don't generally serve the staff.'

I was about to snap something rather unkind, when The Bishop reminded me of his presence by saying, 'Mine. Now do it at once, please.' Then he turned to me. 'I imagine, Euphemia, you have guessed something of what has transpired, though how I do not know. It was most kind of you to help this man, but I do not think you need trouble yourself further. I will do what needs to be done.'

'There has been a tragic accident. At least, I don't believe such a thing would've been done on purpose. But, still, it happened by his own hand. So, what'll happen to him? Oh, dear,' said the waiter. 'Forgive me. I shouldn't comment on a member, but he was such a lovely old gent. One of the old guard. Always tipped generously, did Mr Lovelock.'

The Bishop, quicker than I on the uptake here, said 'Am I to take it that there is some question as to whether or not this poor man took his own life?'

'I wouldn't like to believe so, sir,' said the waiter looking up at The Bishop with worried eyes as if he suddenly remembered who he was talking with. 'No, no, I'm sure it was nothing more than a tragic accident. Even so, I worry about the circumstances, and the consequences.'

'I am not one to judge,' said The Bishop. 'I will say a prayer for his soul and allow our Creator, in His great mercy, to gather our departed brother to Him.'

The Bishop tapped me on the shoulder and took a step back. 'It does look as if we may have to postpone our luncheon. I think things may be a little more complicated than they appear. But it's nothing to worry your head over, my dear. Please go back to your mother, she will be anxious - as I am sure your fiancé will be.'

I smiled at him. I thought it sweet he would try to protect me. 'Whatever occurred, if there is no suicide note and no suspicious circumstances, it will be up to the clergyman of his home village to determine if he is to be buried in sacred ground. If not, he could always be buried on his family's estate, although I believe most clergy are as generous as they can be. Are they not, Step-pa?'

The Bishop's eyebrows rose even higher, but he only said, 'Indeed, my step-daughter is quite correct - if suicide is confirmed the individual can always be buried on their own estate.'

I fancied I could feel his gaze burning into the back of my neck. When I turned to face him, he did not appear hostile, but his expression was one that I am sure had put the fright into many a chorister.

'I'll go back to my mother, shall I?' I said. It wasn't so much as my courage had failed me, but I had the impression that The Bishop was a lot sharper than the people I was used to dealing with. He had, without doubt, already gleaned that my experience must be out of the ordinary for a young lady. Hopefully, if I retreated now he would put it down to bad breeding accrued while working as a servant, a flaw that could easily be ironed out by my forthcoming marriage.

The waiter lifted his face out of the napkin. His face, now wrinkled and reddened, looked like an aged berry.

'Thank you, miss,' he said. 'There's not many as would have cared for how I felt. You're just like Mr Lovelock.' He ended on a sob and plunged his face back down into the napkin. I took the opportunity to flee.

At the table I found Richenda had been located and had not merely drawn up a chair but had procured fresh tea for everyone and a plate of macaroons. Joe was eying her with blatant admiration. There were traces of sugar all down his front. Even my mother, sipping from her tea-cup, looked at my employer approvingly.

'Euphemia,' said my mother, 'where have you been, and what have you done now?'

'Nothing. I merely found the poor man a seat and sent for brandy.' I sat down wondering why I could face off against villains and foreign agents, yet my mother still made me feel as if I was eight years old.

'Where is Bertram?' said Richenda. 'He's not mixed up in all of this, is he?'

'I don't see how,' I said.

'One never knows with you two,' said Richenda darkly.

'It is unfortunate,' said my mother, 'but at a Gentlemen's Club with such elderly members - I do not mean The Bishop, of course.'

'Naturally,' said Richenda.

My mother nodded approvingly again. 'With such elderly members, deaths on the premises must occur now and again. It is our misfortune that it happened today.'

'Positively inconvenient,' I muttered under my breath.

'Euphemia!' snapped my mother.

'Yes, what is it, Mama?' I said straightening my spine swiftly.

'Where is that beau of yours?'

At this point we heard the door open and Bertram

walked into the room. Whatever had occurred had not kept him from his ablutions. He now looked dapper enough that I felt proud of him. I rose as he came across to us. As he drew alongside me he naturally slipped his arm around my waist. Richenda gave a coy little smile and lowered her gaze. My mother assumed the expression of a Gorgon.

'Mother,' I said, 'may I introduce my fiancée, Mr Bertram Stapleford of White Orchards and Stapleford Hall.'

Bertram leaned over and stretched out his hand. 'I am delighted to meet you, ma'am,' he said without any betrayal of the embarrassment I had expected him to show. Richenda must have noticed this because she couldn't resist throwing out, 'Euphemia's mother is actually the Lady Mrs Philomena Hawthorn. Her father is an Earl. Our Euphemia is actually an Honourable. Who would have thought it?'

'It's Mrs Hawthorn or Lady Philomena,' corrected my mother. 'You cannot combine the two forms of address.'

'How very interesting,' said Richenda. 'I don't think I have ever quite got the hang of titles. You must instruct me, Philomena. You did say I could call you Philomena the last time we met, didn't you?'

My mother had the grace to very, very faintly blush.

Bertram squeezed my waist to get my attention and whispered in my ear. 'We need to get going, darling. It seems the old codger might have taken his own life. We don't want to get mixed up in anything. Especially not with your family here. I take it they know nothing about…?' Even though only I could hear him, Bertram did not name the Official Secrets Act - a new-fangled document which promised death as a traitor if mentioned to anyone who hadn't also signed it - nor that we had both been, on more than one occasion, 'assets for the Crown'.

'My thoughts exactly,' I whispered back, trying to make it look as if we were exchanging sweet nothings. 'The Bishop has already requested the doorman to find us somewhere else. I am all for getting out of here as soon as possible, even if we merely decamp to a local Lyon's. There must be one nearby.'

'Agreed,' said Bertram. 'We can always say we want to get your mother and brother away from here. The Bishop can follow on. No point mentioning my sister. A moment's acquaintance would show she has the nerves of a rhinoceros.'

I smothered a giggle. Turning to the table I said, 'Mother, we were thinking, if The Bishop is held up by things, it would be a good idea to take Joe out of here. We could find a nearby tearoom. They might even be able to provide us with sandwiches, although I fear our luncheon will have to be postponed.'

My mother considered this request. 'I don't know.'

'Sandwiches,' said Joe in a hopeful voice.

I took the chance while they debated to whisper to Bertram. 'You are not upset by my station?'

'I do believe the joke is wearing a little thin,' said Bertram. 'But I hope you think I have taken it in good part. I mean, your mother looks most respectable, I could almost believe it were true.'

My face must have betrayed me because Bertram's arm dropped from around my waist. 'You mean it is true?' said Bertram. 'You have been deceiving me all these years? Next you will be telling me you are an heiress!'

I found I could not look him in the face and dropped my gaze.

'You mean that is true too?' His face was a mask of

37

horror.

'We will be able to use it to shore up more of White Orchards,' I said lightly.

'Never,' said Bertram vehemently.

Before I could frame a suitable answer, my mother rose. 'Husband,' she called, for The Bishop had entered the room once more and was crossing the distance between us with fast, loping strides. He arrived in a moment, only slightly breathless.

'There has been a call on the telephone apparatus. It is apparently of the greatest urgency.'

'Here we go,' said Bertram under his breath. Out loud he said, 'I take it the machine is at the front desk.'

'The call is not for you,' said The Bishop. 'It is for Euphemia.'

'What have you done?' said my mother angrily. 'I should have known you would find a way to sabotage our luncheon.'

Chapter Four
Euphemia Gets a Most Vexatious Telephone Call

My hand shook as I picked up the receiver. Bertram stood behind me, brooding even more because I had been the one called to the telephone and not him. The Bishop stood a little way off awaiting any 'development of matters' as he called it. Joe, a macaroon clenched in each hand, was the only one who wasn't obviously angry with me. Richenda had refused to be left on her own and was exhibiting the usual hostility she felt when a situation removed her from cake. I put the receiver to my ear. The person on the other end of the line must have heard me breathing because before I even said a word, they spoke.

'Good morning, my dear. You do have a knack for being in interesting places.'

'It's you,' I said, recognising Fitzroy's voice.

'You sound so delighted to hear from me,' he said.

'No,' I said.

'No what?'

'No, I will not do whatever it is you want me to do. My family and I are about to leave.'

'Ah, that would be a pity,' said Fitzroy. 'But I'm not going to ask you to do anything - except stay there.'

'Why?'

'Now really, Euphemia, when have I ever explained my plans to you?'

'Never,' I said bitterly.

I heard a dry chuckle at the other end of the line. 'It is usually for your own protection. However, this time, as you are in a respectable Gentlemen's Club, for once, I must seek Bertram's aid. My speaking to you is merely a courtesy. If you would be so good as to put your fiancé on the line. And do ask your very lovely family to step into the other room while we speak. He is not as naturally cautious as you are.'

'You can see us?'

'My dear girl, if I could see you, I would be there. I am on my way, but it may take me some time to extricate myself from my current situation. I need you to do something for me. Your mother is a furiously inquisitive person, although you may not have realised it. Giles will have accompanied her as he feels responsible for - well most things really. I expect that comes from being a bishop. I assume your mother brought Joe with her as well? What I need you to do is keep them as far removed from the situation as possible. Just corral them for me, will you?

A thousand retorts crowded on the edge of my tongue. Fitzroy had no business whatsoever prying into what my mother is like. How dare he? And did he know The Bishop? He has a habit of calling people he hasn't even met by their first name, as if he thinks he understands them. But, occasionally, people I have met did indeed know him - although they rarely ever knew him as Fitzroy. I was one of the only people to know that Fitzroy was a codename he had chosen based on an imaginary persona he had invented for himself during an exceptionally lonely childhood. Another dry chuckle broke into my thoughts.

'I hate to rush you, my dearest Euphemia, but time may be of the essence.' I felt myself blush crimson at the continuing endearments. It was quite out of character. All I could think was he was trying to rattle me, but I couldn't think why.

'He wants to speak to you,' I said, holding out the receiver to Bertram.

'He?' said Bertram in a resigned voice.

I nodded. Bertram heaved an enormous sigh as he reached for the phone. 'Bloody -'

I cut him off by saying to the others, 'I think the rest of us should retire to a table. My mother will not find it suitable, but I suspect we will be here for some time.' There was no reason to mention Fitzroy's name to them. Hopefully they would never meet.

Once we were seated I was besieged by questions. Only Richenda kept quiet. She contented herself with giving me what I initially took as an expression of indigestion but what I eventually worked out was meant to be a hard stare. She had suspected before that Bertram, Rory, and I were 'mixed up in something'. Once she realised that she would never be told what was happening, she reluctantly forbore to ask questions as long as she was involved in some of the action. However, this all came too close to home on more than one occasion, although during our last adventure, our connections ended up saving those she loved.[8] Last time she had even met Fitzroy, briefly, although if she thought anything, I suspected she assumed he was with the police. In short, it meant Richenda knew there was no point in asking me questions. Unhappily, my mother and Little Joe were proving indefatigable.

'My dear,' said The Bishop loudly, after twenty minutes of headache-inspiring altercations, 'for whatever

---

[8]Although, in truth, we had to make some very hard choices that Bertram, Rory and I all hope she will never uncover.

reason, I think Euphemia has made it quite clear that she will not be divulging who was on the telephone.'

'But, Husband, I am her mother. What higher authority can a daughter possibly owe allegiance to?'

'You ask that of a bishop, my dear?' said The Bishop with raised eyebrows. 'But in this particular instance I think we can assume Euphemia has not been called upon to perform God's work - although one never knows, he does work in mysterious ways. Regardless, I am convinced she is not able to answer us, is that correct, Euphemia?'

'I am sorry, my Lord,' I said, feeling we were sliding back onto to formal terms, 'but I simply cannot.' To my surprise The Bishop patted me lightly on the sleeve.

'Then I suggest we leave at once,' said my mother. 'There is no point staying here. There is no luncheon and it seems there will be little in the way of communication with my daughter.' Her face set into a mulish look that I knew only too well. If I had been but five years younger I would have been sent to my room without supper for a week. The fact I was now an independent young woman, or as independent as the times allowed, made my mother exceedingly cross. 'Come, Joe. Come, Husband. We shall leave at once.'

The Bishop, who had been standing, sat down in obvious contradiction of my mother's instructions. Joe gave an involuntary gasp but looked impressed. It was clear there was more mettle in The Bishop than either he or I had suspected. 'That seems a little harsh, my dear,' said The Bishop gently. 'We have, only minutes ago, learned of the unexpected death of a member of this establishment -'

'I don't see what that has to do with it,' broke in my mother.

The Bishop neither raised his hand to interrupt her, nor spoke over her. He merely stared directly at her in a manner not hostile, but like that of a clergyman who is waiting for his congregation to quieten down so he may begin his sermon.[9] To my astonishment I heard my mother's voice peter out. 'The point, my dear, is that I doubt whether the poor gentleman in question left his house with even the slightest consideration that this was to be his last day on earth. I, on the other hand, being of the clergy, am a constant usher for births and deaths. I know our time upon this earth is short. None of us know what tomorrow will bring. And so I am loath, ever, to let a family part on terms of discord. Especially when it is my own family. Besides, it has been made clear to us, with utmost politeness, that we may all be here for some time.'

My mother made a noise that from anyone else might have been a snorting humph, but which we all decided as one to take as a sigh.

'I am well aware that you have missed your daughter desperately since she was forced to leave your home,' continued my step-pa (this was how I was thinking of him again). 'I am also aware that the sibling bond between Euphemia and Joe is very strong. I believe it would upset him considerably to take him away from his sister once more.'

'Yes, it would,' piped up Joe. 'For you, Effie, I'll even miss luncheon.' At this point I had to hug him, and if my eyes brimmed with tears for a moment I took care no one else saw.

---

[9]My father could do exactly the same thing with his congregation, although he could never get it to work on my mother.

'I suppose we could stay a little while. At least until that fiancé of yours comes back. If he ever does, of course.'

The Bishop gave a stern look and my mother actually blushed and lowered her eyes. Today was indeed a day of miracles. It was also another day to be annoyed with Fitzroy yet again. How dare he place me in such a position? Then I remembered that however annoying I found the spy, he only ever called in civilian assets when he had no other choice. He might enjoy my being irritated on occasion, but he would never instigate any serious action unless it was necessary.

'Has the waiter gone?' I asked.

'I think they have been quite clear about the situation regarding food,' said Richenda sadly.

I shook my head. 'I wanted to know more about the gentleman who died,' I said.

'Why?' said The Bishop.

I was struggling to think of a good answer when Bertram came back into the room. Following him came several waiters bearing trays of sandwiches, bowls of soup, side plates of salad and a selection of cakes. Richenda's mouth puckered into an 'O' of delighted surprise and Joe let out a squeak of pleasure.

No one spoke while the waiters rearranged some tables, seated us and laid out the fare. Bertram contrived to get the seat next to mine. 'Under the circumstances,' he said to the table, 'I suggested the kitchen could, at the very least, create a light luncheon. There will be tea, coffee, and petit fours afterwards.'

'And what are the circumstances?' inquired The Bishop. Another waiter appeared with carafes of water, fruit juice, and wine. The Bishop graciously accepted a glass of Beaujolais. 'I do feel this year's has a slight banana flavour,' he said. 'But one cannot have everything.' Bertram and I also took wine. I'm sure Joe would also have done so if he thought he could have got away with it. Richenda and my mother took only water. During this flurry of beverages, Bertram managed to whisper to me, 'Fitzroy wants -'

'You were saying?' said The Bishop. The waiters left.

'Ah, yes, well. Bit of an extraordinary thing really. It turns out the poor man who died is, well, a friend of a friend of ours.'

'So, it was this friend on the telephone?' said The Bishop. 'Only it did not seem to me that Euphemia felt on friendly terms with him.'

'Yes, well,' said Bertram. 'He's more of a pal of mine. We've known each other a while. You know how it is, my Lord, when the lady in your life doesn't always get on with your previous pals.'

'The Bishop is acquainted with only the best people,' said my mother frostily.

'Not all of whom you favour,' said The Bishop lightly. 'Although you are always gracious, my love.'

My mother paused, untangling the compliment from the comment.

'This friend must be quite elderly?' said The Bishop.

Bertram took a big swig of wine. 'No, actually, he's around my age. You see, his father was very close to the chap who's died. Made him my friend's godfather. Rather like a second father and all that.' Bertram quickly shoved half a ham sandwich in his mouth before anyone could ask him anything else.

'And your friend wants you to do what precisely?'

'Oh, nothing really. He's asked that I keep an eye on

45

things until he can get here. He is his godfather's executor, and the old chap had some particular things he wanted done upon his demise.'

'Like?' asked Joe excitedly.

'Oh, you know, this and that,' said Bertram waving an arm around and almost knocking over a decanter of wine. I managed to catch it. 'My friend just wants everything kept as is, until he can get here.'

'And how long will that be?' said my mother.

Bertram tugged at his collar. 'I'm not exactly sure,' he said. 'There is absolutely no reason for you and the Bish to hang about...' he paused as my mother gave him her most deadly stare. 'I mean The Bishop, of course. Nor Master Joe. I'd appreciate it if you could take my sister to the train station. There's a station close to her husband's estate. I can make arrangements from here for someone to pick her up.'

'And Euphemia?' asked my mother.

'I will run her back in my motor later,' said Bertram. 'As you have no doubt become aware, we have one or two things to discuss.'

'You mean how she's an Honourable and you're not,' said Joe.

My mother gave him a quick box on the ears for his language.

'Among other things, yes,' said Bertram with a quiet dignity I found admirable. His cover story for Fitzroy might be ragged, to say the least, but I thought he was behaving admirably. Although I had noticed that there had been a consistent expression of him looking into things alone. I assumed this was only until my mother left.

'I cannot possibly leave you here with Euphemia without a chaperone,' said my mother.

46

Bertram looked pointedly around the room where waiters skulked in discreet corners, or behind pot plants.

'Servants cannot guarantee a girl's virtue,' said my mother.

'I can assure you Euphemia has been in plenty of situations alone with my brother,' said Richenda, and then obviously realising how it sounded, 'and has never come to any harm. Bertram is a consummate gentleman and I will take serious offence with anyone who says otherwise.' She sat back in her chair looking as formidable as one can when they do not know they have cream on their upper lip.

'You are all forgetting that the establishment has asked me to say some words over the departed,' said The Bishop. 'Perhaps I should do that now.'

'Ah, yes, then I had better come with you,' said Bertram getting to his feet.

'To ensure the deceased's last wishes are kept?' said The Bishop.

'Exactly,' said Bertram.

The Bishop unfolded himself from his chair. 'And to be clear, those are…?'

'Complicated,' said Bertram. 'I won't bore you with them. But I'll be on hand if…'

'Anything needs to be arranged,' said The Bishop, raising his eyebrows.

'Exactly,' said Bertram.

He bent down to give me a kiss on the cheek, inadvertently scandalising my mother. 'Why does he have to be so tall,' he whispered in my ear.

I watched them leave the room with a mixture of feelings. None of them were pleasurable. Fitzroy couldn't possibly have meant Bertram to take on this situation alone. Aside from the fact my beloved had a dicky heart, and would be facing unknown dangers alone, it went against my principles to be excluded - after all, Fitzroy had recruited me first. Why, he'd even said he only allowed Bertram and Rory to join our activities because we came as part of a package. Rory might have bailed on Bertram, but I had no intention of doing so.

Chapter Five
Richenda Does Her Bit

Little Joe ate sandwich after sandwich without a word, but his bright eyes watched me closely. My mother sipped her glass of water, but the cucumber sandwich on her plate remained untouched. Her gaze rarely wandered from my face. I had to put my wine glass back on the table as I was concerned I might snap the stem under pressure from my fingers, I felt so tense. How the devil was I to get away?

'Euphemia,' said Richenda suddenly. All eyes turned to her. 'I do not feel quite well. Could you accompany me to the powder room? I may wish to loosen...' She looked at Joe who was staring at her intently. 'Something,' she finished.

'Of course,' I said rising at once.

My mother's gaze flickered between us.

'I am beginning to wonder if I might once again be in an *interesting situation*,' said Richenda directly to my mother while placing one hand on her abdomen.

My mother, being of the generation when such things remained unmentioned, gestured to us to leave at once.[10]

Once we were out of the room. 'Really, Richenda?' I said. 'I thought you and Hans...' I faltered. 'Oh, but this is delightful.'

---

[10]Sometimes I wonder how my parents managed to have children, but I believe this is quite normal. No child ever believes that they parents were ever intimate - and I am quite happy to leave the situation there.

Richenda, who has a quicker intellect than anyone ever credits her with, led me unerringly through the maze of corridors to the powder room. Once we were inside she checked for company and then sat down heavily in an armchair. 'Goodness, Euphemia. You are meant to be the smart one. Of course I'm not in the family way. Hans and I are hardly speaking, let alone...'

I could feel heat rising to my face. 'Then why?'

'It was merely a ruse to get you out of there,' said Richenda. 'I could see you were on the verge of exploding when you realised The Bishop and Bertram were going off together, and without you.' She snorted. 'And as for his story, whoever was on the end of the telephone apparatus,' she held up her hand, 'no, I'm not asking, but whoever it was cannot be very bright if they think Bertram can handle things on his own. He made a right hash of that story. A simple-minded rabbit would not have believed it.'

I sank down into another chair. 'You are very acute,' I said.

'Don't worry, I will not bother asking any awkward questions. I never did figure out what you, Bertram, and McLeod were up to, but I have decided that as you and my brother are people of good conscience, I should assist you. Hence my claiming to need your help. You are now free to join Bertram and the "Bish". I must say, I rather like that as a nickname for him.'

'You don't know my mother. She'll come after me.'

'Not immediately. I'll wait here a while. By the time I go back hopefully you and Bertram will have managed to discuss whatever is needed. I only ask for one thing...'

'Which is?' I said. 'Please don't ask me to speak to Hans for you. I don't...'

'Believe me when I say the very last thing I want you

to do for me is speak to Hans,' said Richenda with an acidity that surprised me.

'Have I done something to upset you?' I said, confused. 'I am very grateful for the escape from my mother.'

Richenda shook her head and heaved a big sigh. 'No, you have done nothing. It is Hans. As far as he is concerned, you are the perfect woman incarnate, and would have made him an ideal wife - unlike me.'

'Oh no, that cannot be true,' I said.

Richenda gave a sniff. 'Leave it alone, Euphemia. I've always known Hans didn't love me. It was a marriage of convenience. And you do always behave perfectly - although now I know why, you were brought up to act like a lady. My mother never bothered about such things and my stepmother would have happily seen me drown in a pond. I will have to do better. I am hoping that when you are married, Hans will see sense and that we both have to make the best of the bargain we've made.'

Richenda pulled a handkerchief from her sleeve and blew her nose violently. 'No, all I was going to say was if there is anything I can do to help in whatever you're doing, just let me know. I like to feel useful. It rarely happens, but I have helped you and Bertram before, have I not?'

'Yes, you have,' I said.

'Then if I can help, please call on me again. It would be good to take my mind off other things.'

I nodded and hesitated. I hated to see Richenda so upset. We had truly become friends, but it seemed the sooner I was married and away from her home the better it would be for her.

'Please go,' said Richenda. 'You're wasting time.'

I nodded again and left without a word. Richenda had

been keen to hand over the reins of responsibility to me when I was her companion. I should never have allowed her to do so. I knew Hans had had a *tendre* for me, but I also knew he was an honourable man. However, having another woman perform the greater majority of the duties expected of your wife had not helped their marriage. I would have to speak to Bertram about it.

I turned in the opposite direction to the coffee lounge. I didn't know where to go but heading further into the gentlemen's domain seemed a good way to start. I had no doubt that any attempts to keep the situation quiet would only be met by inquisitive members.

I heard voices in the distance and moved towards them, taking care to keep my footsteps as quiet as possible. I heard Bertram's voice as I came to a corner in the passageway. I peeped around the edge and saw Bertram, The Bishop, and a man in a steward's outfit, standing by a large oak door that terminated this hallway. There were no seats or potted plants along the corridor, so absolutely no cover for me to hide behind if I wanted to get closer. They had their backs to me, but I couldn't count on them not turning around at any moment - much in the way one plays that game as a child. Instead I had to content myself with staying put. I couldn't hear properly, but I could see, and when they opened the door to enter a room, I might be able to glimpse inside. Better yet, I might even manage to sneak closer, if they were otherwise occupied.

Bertram spoke again. I couldn't make out what he was saying, but I understood the tone. He was attempting to explain that he had the authority to visit the deceased. This was answered by polite intonations of the steward, who clearly had no intention of letting him in. Then I heard The Bishop. I barely recognised his voice. He said something short and commanding. The next sound I heard was that of a key engaging with a lock. The door swung open and the three of them walked in. I crept cautiously forward. Luck favoured me. It was clearly a small room and they left the door open. Although The Bishop was tall, he was lean. Neither Bertram or the steward were of any great height, so as they moved, or rather shuffled, out of each other's way, I was able to see inside the room. A long window looked out onto a garden. In front of it stood a wide desk. Pulled up to this was what I believe they call a captain's chair, wooden with a low back, and which can swivel, the kind much favoured by some writers. In this chair, and half over the desk, was slumped a man.

Nothing about the way he lay looked odd and yet I knew beyond doubt he was dead. In my time I have seen many corpses and I can only say that, to my eyes, the absence of spirit leaves an emptiness that no slumbering or fainted form ever conveys. I leaned back against the wall, trying to keep out of sight. I felt a little faint. Unwanted memories of the nightmarish scenes I had had to contend with when I searched for Fitzroy's body threatened to overwhelm me.[11] That night aboard the *Carpathia* still haunted me. Only Hans and Richenda had shared some of that experience, and they had not been required to inspect the dead.

I took several deep breaths. I will not faint, I told myself. From the other end of the hallway I heard a low murmur of voices. If I didn't make my move soon I would lose my chance.

---

[11]At the time it was believed he might have been dead, but as evidenced by the earlier telephone conversation, he was very much alive. He is rather annoying like that.

Lifting my skirts scandalously high above my ankles[12] I moved forward as quickly as I could with as little sound as possible. Fitzroy had shown me a long time ago how to move with minimal sound. However, to do this perfectly, one has to take one's time. Time, in this particular instance, was one thing I did not have. Moving more rapidly than I would have liked, I was still able to muffle the noise of my approach, and my hope was that the three men were sufficiently distracted by the body in the room to notice. I managed to get to the doorway and flatten myself along the side without anyone noticing.

'It's a very sad affair,' said a voice I did not know, but which I presumed to be the steward's. 'But Mr Lovelock was one of our older members.'

'I take it he was a long-term member?' said Bertram.

'Yes, sir.'

'Well liked?' asked Bertram.

'I couldn't answer for the other members, sir,' said the unhelpfully discreet steward, 'but he never gave the staff any problems. Always said good morning and what not. Tipped well at Christmas.'

'Did he often come in to the club?' said Bertram.

'On most days, sir.'

I could almost feel Bertram's frustration. The steward, for his own reasons, appeared to be giving the briefest answers possible. Bertram would be thinking that a long list of questions would arouse The Bishop's suspicion, and while Fitzroy wanted him only to preserve the scene, we both knew that the spy would expect Bertram to do some

---

[12]Have you ever tried to move quietly in long skirts? Then do not moralise at me.

54

groundwork while memories and impressions were still fresh. And also, of course, to close down the building should it prove to be more than a natural death. I wracked my brains for what Bertram had told us. It had been some claptrap about the dead man wanting things done a certain way. All he had managed to say to me was that 'Fitzroy wants'. Wanted what?

'The Lord calls us all to him in the end,' said The Bishop in a respectful and mournful tone. 'Does he leave family?'

'I couldn't say, my lord,' said the less than helpful steward. I imagined I could hear Bertram grinding his teeth.

'Did you lock the door?' asked The Bishop.

'Err, no,' said the steward. 'The door was locked when the waiter brought Mr Lovelock his soup. He always has - had - soup at the same time every day. He said it helped him to keep to his schedule.'

'Schedule?' said Bertram, almost too eagerly.

'He liked things done in a certain way,' said the steward.

'So I believe,' said The Bishop, his tone dry.

'Err, yes, exactly,' said Bertram. 'That's why I'm here. To ensure things are done a certain way.'

'You appear to be attempting to shield part of the desk with your body,' observed The Bishop. 'As I assured your colleague, I am not here to judge.'

I heard sounds of movement as they shuffled places. 'Ah,' said Bertram. 'I see. That may well explain everything.'

I willed him with every ounce of my being to say more.

'I see,' said The Bishop. 'Was this a long-term...?' He broke off.

'It's very common with gentlemen of his age,' said the porter. 'He said it helped him focus.'

'Focus?' said Bertram. I could tell he was desperate to know more, but I thought he was doing a jolly good job of not asking leading questions. It was all so very different from the first case we had tackled.

'Yes, sir. He was writing his memoirs. Every weekday he booked this room between ten a.m. and three p.m. to work on them. Like many of our members, he once held high office.'

'How interesting,' said The Bishop. 'Which?'

'I'm sorry?' said the steward.

'Which was his high office?'

'Oh, the diplomatic service, sir. He retired six months ago and has been writing his memoirs ever since.'

That, I thought, made perfect sense. He must have been writing something that Fitzroy wanted to read before it met with scrutiny from a wider audience. We were poised on the edge of a potential war and the indiscreet writings of a civil servant in the wrong hands could, in a worst-case scenario, tip the balance into outright conflict. Although I thought it was more likely that he had written about the indiscretions of others in high office. Fitzroy, no doubt, intended to do a little editing. He had doubtless put a watch on Lovelock and this was why he had been apprised of the man's death so very quickly. But if he had someone inside the club, why wasn't he dealing with the situation? I very much wanted to discuss the situation with Bertram. There was nothing for it. I would have to reveal myself and face the consequences.

'I think it is about time I did my part,' said The Bishop. I couldn't think what he meant. It was ridiculous to think he would be Fitzroy's man, but then stranger things had happened. I stepped out from my hiding place at the exact moment that The Bishop said, 'Let us pray.'

I could hardly announce my presence now, so feeling a little guilty, I took the opportunity to examine the scene from my position while the others had their eyes shut. Lovelock had curly, snowy white hair. He had slumped upon the desk in such a way that I could not see his features. He was wearing a white shirt, the left sleeve of which was rolled up. From what I could see, I thought his frame to be spare, suggestive that he had been wiry when he was younger, but certainly not frail. The steward had his head bowed, but his body still shielded a small part of the desk. I craned my neck but could not see what was behind him. Whatever it was it had to be quite small. 'And so, Our Heavenly Father, we commend unto your care, the soul of Killian Lovelock, knowing that you will accept him with love and understanding, now that he enters a better world,' continued The Bishop. His praying voice was distinctly melodious as he finished off with the Lord's Prayer. It tugged at me to join in the prayer, as my father had taught me from an early age. I found myself silently mouthing the words and it was then that I realised what was so wrong with the scene.

'Amen,' said The Bishop.

'Amen,' said Bertram and the steward in unison.

'Where,' I said, 'are his memoirs?'

The three of them turned as one to stare at me. Their shocked faces berated my intrusion.

'Look,' I said, pointing at the desk, 'there isn't a single sheet of paper evident. Someone else must have been here.'

Chapter Six
Everyone is Cross With Me

'Euphemia!' said The Bishop. 'This is not a sight for a young lady.'

'Miss, you cannot be here,' said the steward. 'Ladies are not allowed in the members' rooms.'

'Dammit, you're right, Euphemia,' said Bertram. 'Where are the wretched things?'

'I expect, sir,' said the steward, who by now was rigid with disapproval, 'that Mr Lovelock put them away as he was expecting soup. In our professional experience, soup and paperwork do not go well together. The members even wrote a by-law about it.'

'Where?' I said. 'Where did he put them?'

'I have no idea, miss. Now, if you wouldn't mind, I must insist you return…'

'And if he was expecting soup, why did he lock the door?' I said.

'Ah, well, Euphemia,' said The Bishop. 'I don't think we need to go into that, but the gentleman did have a reason. Let us leave it at that.'

'What reason?' I asked. I looked directly at Bertram, who avoided my gaze. 'Leave it, Euphemia,' he said. 'There was a reason. Trust me.'

'Fine,' I said feeling irritated. 'You won't tell me the reason. I presume due to the fear of damaging my delicate female sensibilities. Although, Bertram, you of all people should know the unladylike events I have been exposed to.' The Bishop gave me a strange look and the steward's eyes fairly bulged from his head. 'But where are the papers?'

'I expect, miss,' said the steward, 'they are in the desk.'

'Then we should look,' I said.

'Euphemia, as you can see, we cannot open the drawers of the desk without moving Mr Lovelock,' said The Bishop.

'Then move him,' I said. 'Bertram, you know I am right.'

'I suppose we should check they are all in order,' said Bertram. 'It is the kind of thing that I was asked to do.'

'We cannot move him until the doctor has confirmed he is dead,' said the steward.

'I do not think there can be any doubt of that,' said The Bishop. He addressed Bertram. 'If you believe it is completely necessary then I am sure between the three of us we can respectfully move Mr Lovelock to check his papers are secure. I can understand that the executor would want you to ensure they are safe. Especially considering his career.'

'We should also check him for the room key,' I said. 'I presume that there is a master.'

The put-upon steward nodded. Then he blurted out, 'But we simply can't move the body with a lady in the room, sirs. It is not right.'

'I quite agree,' said The Bishop. 'Euphemia will return to her mother. It is unfortunate that she became lost and stumbled upon this distressing sight. However, I am sure we can rely on her discretion.' He looked at me. 'You may not know it, my dear, but you need some hot, sweet tea. You are as white as a sheet. This is obviously a severe shock for you.'

'I have seen worse,' I said. 'I was on the *Carpathia*.'

'I am sorry,' said The Bishop, 'this must bring back many unhappy memories of that terrible tragedy. No wonder you are looking so pale. Perhaps you should escort her back, Mr Stapleford?'

A conflict of emotions visibly crossed Bertram's face. I could only guess at some of them, but I did spot genuine annoyance. 'I need to stay here,' said Bertram firmly. 'Euphemia, your stepfather is right. You cannot be here while we move the body.'

'Bertram,' I said in astonishment. 'Surely you…'

'I am firm on this,' said Bertram, pursing his lips. 'There are many reasons you have been allowed latitude during your career, Euphemia, but on this I stand firm.'

'You forget,' I said, 'I am no longer your servant to command.'

'Indeed I do not,' said Bertram hotly. 'I am now all too aware that for the duration of our acquaintance you have been my social superior.'

'I have never claimed to be any such thing,' I said.

'No, you simply kept your origins from me for several years,' said Bertram.

'I did not realise it would be such a problem,' I said, 'for you to accept me as I truly am.'

The Bishop gently took my arm, but I shook him off. 'Do you have a problem with me as well?' I said.

'Euphemia, leave this room at once,' said Bertram. 'I demand it.'

'You have no right to demand anything of me,' I said. 'I have every right to be here. Why, I was involved with…'

'My Lord, please escort Miss St John - I mean Miss Martins, from the room. This man and I will manage.' Bertram cut me off not a moment too soon. I realised I had been about to go too far.

'I am sorry, Bertram,' I said.

'As am I,' said Bertram. 'I will not expect you to return my ring. You may keep it as a token of happier days.' Then he turned to discuss moving the body with the porter.

Once again The Bishop took my arm. This time I did not protest. Indeed, I needed the support. My legs shook beneath me.

'Come along, Euphemia,' said The Bishop. 'It is a difficult time for everyone.'

I made no reply. My vision swam, and I could hear my heart beating loudly in my ears. If I did not sit down shortly I suspected I would faint. I made no answer to my stepfather. I leaned heavily on his arm, while he continued to say soothing phrases and attempted to assure me all would be well. But I knew that everything was wrong. Bertram no longer loved me. In that moment I cared nothing for my duty to the nation, Fitzroy and his interference, or my mother's approval. All that mattered was the truth, that Bertram could only love me as he had previously known me - a lowly servant. As an independent and titled young lady I meant nothing to him.

'Oh, pooh,' said Richenda as she poured me a cup of tea. 'They probably did not want you to see that the man had soiled himself. I believe most people do when they die. It is as if everything suddenly lets go.'

'Oh,' I said. I was sitting a little apart with her. The Bishop was deep in conversation with my mother and little Joe was doing his best to make an aeroplane out of his starched napkin.

'Was there a smell?' asked Richenda. 'The twins' underthings… Oh, my goodness, I cannot tell you what a shock it was when I walked in on Nanny changing them one day. I though the poor little angels were dying. Apparently, it was all perfectly normal.' She helped herself from a small plate of sandwiches that were stacked at her side. 'I expect they felt they were preserving the fellow's dignity by not moving him when you were there.'

I sipped my tea. 'Why did they not simply say?'

'Say such a thing to a young and innocent unmarried girl? Why, I'll wager your mother chased you from the room when your father died, did she not?'

I nodded.

'Same thing I expect. Respect for the dead and all that. Relatives generally do not get to see them until they are properly cleaned up. How interesting that you can have been around so much death and have not come to know this.' She popped another sandwich in her mouth.

'Bertram does not love me,' I said. I managed to suppress the sob that rose in my throat.

'What rot,' said Richenda. 'This has been a bit of a trying day for him, that is all. I mean it's understandable he's a bit miffed that you didn't tell him the truth about yourself. I quite see why you didn't tell us - I mean Richard and me - but you were, *are*, engaged to Bertram. That has to sting a bit.' She lifted her cup, but then paused. 'Hans didn't know, did he?'

I shook my head. In truth Hans had suspected, but I had never confirmed it.

Richenda slurped her tea, appearing happy with my answer. 'I think it might have been no more than a minor tiff had you not made that comment about using your money to repair his estate. Bit of a double blow, that. He's awfully proud about not taking money from anyone - including our father's estate. I know he got the money to buy the house from his godfather's estate, but at least that was clean money, not blood money like ours.' She picked up another sandwich and inspected its edges. 'I do believe I should send for more. These are beginning to curl in the heat. But no decent man wants to live off his wife.' She patted my arm. Richenda never had a light touch, and it was akin to being pawed by a large friendly dog. 'Don't worry, Euphemia. It'll all be all right. Bertram is a bit on edge about everything. I expect he feels a fool in front of your mother too - I know you didn't mean to do that to him, but right now he's not thinking straight. Believe me, I know what a loveless match looks like and yours most certainly isn't one. He'll come around once he's calmed down - and once we are out of this wretched place. Why, do you know, they don't even have any cake available!'

I sat there rather stupidly letting her prattle on. Perhaps, I thought, she will let me continue to work for her, or would that be too awkward? It would be lovely to see little Joe every day, but I did not think I could manage to live once again with my mother. If nothing else, she would make it her business to marry me off as quickly as possible. No doubt she would pick suitor after suitor, all of them older than me and positive, steadying influences, until finally I was worn down and ended up marrying a man who looked like a sheep. I hid my face behind my napkin and hiccupped as I tried not to cry.

'Excuse me, miss, but there's another telephone call for you.'

'How exciting,' said Richenda. She looked at my face. 'Would you like me to get them to say you are indisposed? You do not look at all well.'

'No, I will go,' I said and got up. The Bishop and my

mother remained engaged in deep conversation and I had no wish to speak to either. I followed the porter to the telephone. I could feel Richenda's eyes on my back as I left the room, but she had the sense not to ask to accompany me.

I picked up the receiver. 'Yes,' I said.

'It's going to take me longer to get there than I hoped,' said Fitzroy's voice.

'How annoying for you,' I said.

There was a pause at the other end of the line. Then he said, 'Indeed. Can I assume that you have involved yourself in the investigation, or has everything gone smoothly and poor Mr Lovelock has merely succumbed to old age and poor judgement?'

'What do you think?' I said.

'If you could be a little more informative,' said Fitzroy. 'I realise you are attempting to be discreet, but at this point I could do with some actual information.'

'I am going to marry a sheep,' I said, and to my extreme embarrassment I burst into tears.

There was a stunned silence at the other end of the line. Finally, Fitzroy said, 'I wouldn't advise that at all. There is virtually no decent conversation to be had from a sheep.'

My only response was a most curious noise, the combination of a sob and a laugh emerging at the same time.

Silence continued on the other end of the line for some time. Then he said, 'Is it a particular sheep you have in mind?'

I felt a slight twitch at the corner of my mouth. 'I am so sorry,' I managed to say. 'I have had a bit of a disagreement with Bertram. I should not trouble you with it.'

'I would rather you did not,' said Fitzroy, 'although I have to say, I think it a little cruel of you to describe him as a sheep.'

'He isn't the sheep,' I said.

'Glad to hear it,' said Fitzroy. 'Do I take it he is annoyed at your inability to stay out of this?'

'Yes,' I said. 'But more that I didn't tell him who I was.'

'That was only to be expected,' said Fitzroy. 'He'll get over it. Now, tell me what you have seen.'

'I followed them to the room that Lovelock was found in. They believe he wrote his memoirs in there every weekday between ten and three. He booked the room and was in possession of a key. It was locked when they discovered him. They opened the door with the master key.'

'Did he have the key on him?'

'I asked that, but they made me leave the room before they checked, so I do not know.'

Fitzroy swore so violently I felt myself redden from head to foot. I was so shocked I stopped crying. I heard him breathing heavily. Then he said, in what I recognised as a carefully controlled voice, 'Did you push your way into the room where he died? Did you see his body?'

'Yes.'

'Dammit, Euphemia. I didn't want you to see that.'

'It's not like you to consider my sensibilities.'

His response surprised me. 'What you were asked to do on the *Carpathia* was unconscionable for a civilian. I know it affected you profoundly.'

'Thank you,' I said suddenly feeling very pathetic. 'No one else…' I could not find the right words.

'They wouldn't,' said Fitzroy. 'Unfortunately, you are

at the scene and I am not. I have told you more than once that I am not lacking in compassion, but there are times when matters must overrule such concerns. I need you to pull yourself together. I don't want you involved in this case, but it doesn't appear at present as if either of us have any choice.'

In the past Fitzroy had shown me occasional kindness, but this time I heard real regret in his voice over my involvement. 'I understand,' I said in a clearer voice.

'Good girl,' said Fitzroy. 'Now, Lovelock was a heroin addict. I thought it possible he'd overdosed by accident. He'd been taking steadily more and more over the years.'

'That must have been what they were hiding from me,' I said.

'Who? What? Be precise.'

'There was something at the end of his desk that the porter and The Bishop did not want me to see.'

'It's liable to be a small case,' said Fitzroy. 'It would contain primarily a syringe, but there would be other accoutrements. If empty, the case would be of the size to fit inside a medium-sized pocket. Velvet-lined, but with a hard outer shell, like an oversized spectacles case.'

'I can look for it.'

'Tell Bertram to do it. It's liable to be an old-fashioned one. He started taking the drug after a German quack prescribed it late last century. For a cough.'

'You believe he was still taking it?'

'Do you know how it gets its name?'

'No.'

'Because it makes people feel heroic. For an older man with most of his life behind him...'

'Yes, I can understand the appeal,' I said. 'Do you want us to bring in a doctor?'

66

'Not yet. What I really want to be told is that there is nothing odd about his death.'

'Apart from locking himself in his room.'

'Don't be dense, Euphemia.'

'There was no sign of his memoirs in the room.'

Fitzroy swore obscenely again. This time he apologised. 'You couldn't have led with that?' he said.

'I was sent from the room before they searched the desk, so they could be in that. There's a soup by-law, you see -'

Fitzroy spoke over me. 'This is vital,' he said. 'If the memoirs are not in the room then you close down the establishment and prevent anyone from leaving until I get there.'

'You mean?'

'I mean, if they are missing then the chances are this is murder.' He swore again and without apology rang off. I was left holding the receiver in my hand and wondering how on earth we were meant to keep everyone in the building until he arrived. Well, if Bertram didn't want my help he would have to work out how to do it himself.

Chapter Seven
In Which Bertram Shows Initiative

I found Bertram standing outside the dead man's room. He was pale and sweat beaded on his forehead. In the process of wiping his hands thoroughly on his handkerchief he had failed to notice my approach. It occurred to me that although he too had seen a corpse before, this would be the first time he had to handle one.

'Fitzroy called again.'

Bertram started forward. I held up my hand to forestall him. 'He's already rung off. He wanted to know, as I did,' I couldn't help myself from adding this, 'if the key was in Mr Lovelock's pocket.'

'It was,' said Bertram curtly.

'And if the memoirs are there.'

'The desk is locked. We are unable to find the key. I am awaiting a man with tools,' said Bertram.

'Only,' I continued, 'if the papers are not present, he wishes you to close this establishment to all outsiders...

'Of course,' said Bertram interrupting. 'And make a thorough search of the place. I had thought of that.'

'Most importantly,' I said, 'he does not want you to allow anyone to leave.'

'How the hell does he expect me to do that?'

'Bertram,' I said shocked. 'Such language will not help us - I mean you. I will go back to the lounge and sit with my family.'

'Oh no,' said Bertram. 'You cannot leave this all on me. I am only involved with that wretched man because of my relationship with you.'

I sniffed and looked down my nose at him, hoping my eyes were no longer red from crying. 'I was not aware we still had a relationship,' I said.

'Oh, for...' Bertram stopped himself. 'Of course we have a relationship. I'm damned angry with you, but I still love you. God help me.'

My heart leaped inside me. 'I see,' I said coolly. 'Perhaps we can discuss matters between us when things here are resolved. I shall be in the lounge when you are free.'

'What on earth did Fitzroy say to make you suddenly so obedient?' growled Bertram. 'I have never managed to make you do as I ask.'

I merely raised what I hoped was a haughty eyebrow, turned on my heel and walked away. As I turned I couldn't keep a smile from spreading across my face. Bertram still loved me. I did understand his distress at my elevated social status, but I would be the last one to admit that to him.

Back in the lounge I found Richenda toying with her remaining sandwiches and talking to my brother. 'It was at this point,' she was saying, 'that we heard a sound like rolling thunder coming from the other side of the attic. The servants had assured us that there was nothing there but old luggage and unwanted furniture, but what we heard -' She looked up as I approached. 'You are looking much happier,' she said. 'Have you and Bertram sorted things between you?'

'Not yet,' I said. 'But we have agreed that we will.'

'I was telling your brother about our hunt for Hans' mad first wife in the attic,' said Richenda.

Joe turned to me, his eyes bright, 'Is she still there?' he

asked. 'Ranting and raving?'

'Hardly,' I said.

'Don't tell him,' said Richenda. 'I'll finish the story later, Joe. Now, go and see your mother. I am sure she is missing you.'

Joe stood and gave us both a short bow. It was adorable, and I had to sit on my hands not to reach out and hug him. He went off to my mother. 'He is a lovely young man,' said Richenda. 'Beautifully behaved. I am quite surprised you are related.'

I smiled. 'When we lived in the country he was forever falling out of trees and bringing home injured wildlife he had found, to care for. That and putting spiders in the maid's bed. You have all that to look forward to with your children.'

'I hope so,' said Richenda, dubiously. 'Are we able to leave? I am getting bored of this place and I suppose Hans will be wondering where I am. Or he will do as the afternoon wears on. Or possibly not until dinner…'

'Did you not tell him where you were going?' I said.

'No, I walked out after the row. I expect he thought I was going to stomp around the gardens.'

'He will be ever so worried.'

Richenda snorted.

'The very least you can do is ring up Stone and ask him to tell Hans you are safe and well, and will be returning shortly.'

Richenda rolled her eyes. 'And no,' I said. 'I am not ringing up your husband a second time to tell him where you have run off to. Once was enough. Besides, Amy will be asking for you.'

It was this appeal that reached her. 'Oh, very well. Come with me at least. I don't like using those infernal machines.'

However, when we reached the front desk, the porter there regretfully refused to allow us access to the phone. 'I am sorry, ladies, but it is more than my job's worth. I have my orders.'

'From whom?' demanded Richenda, her eyes blazing. Now that she could not use the telephone, she wanted to use it more than anything else.[13]

'Mr Stapleford, Ma'am,' said the porter. 'He's had orders from the Foreign Office.' The porter nodded in a serious way that suggested there was a lot more to this than he was able to tell us.

'How ridiculous,' said Richenda. 'Where is my wretched brother? We'll soon see about this.'

At that moment a tall gentleman, carrying an ebony cane and dressed in an excellent suit, entered the foyer. I gauged him to be in his early forties. His dark hair had begun to grey at the temples and his face had deep frown lines, but for all that he had those saturnine good looks that some females admire. He tipped his hat to us.

'That's me for the day, Evans,' he said to the porter and walked towards the door.

'Mr Prendergast,' said Evans. 'I think…'

'Not now, Evans. On the way to an important meeting,' said Prendergast and reached for the door. It was only then that I realised the doorman was missing. I turned to look at Evans, who tugged uncomfortably at his collar. I looked back at the door. Prendergast pulled and pushed, but the door refused to budge. 'Damn thing is stuck, Evans.

---

[13]Rather like a dog that ignores its bone until you try and take it away, at which time it will do its best to take your arm off.

Where is Walters?'

'On the other side, sir. He's turning people away now that we've closed for the day,' said Evans. I saw his knuckles go white as he gripped the edge of the desk.

'What rot are you talking about, man? Of course the club isn't closed. Not unless you have decided to lock us all in! Ha!'

I pursed my lips to avoid a smile. Bertram had come up with an idea after all. I had to admit it was neat, even if it was liable to antagonise everyone present.

'Mr Stapleford's orders, sir. No one is allowed to leave.'

'Who in perdition's name is Mr Stapleford? I've never heard of the man.'

'He's had orders from the Foreign Office, sir,' said Evans. 'It's to do with Mr Lovelock's sudden demise. Apparently, his memoirs are missing.'

'What the devil has that got to do with anything,' said Prendergast, striding towards the desk. Richenda and I, as one, moved out of his way. 'I have told you I need to leave at once for an urgent meeting,' he said and with that he brought his cane smashing down on the desk to emphasise his point. Richenda jumped. Evans' knuckles went even whiter, but he held his ground.

'It's more than my job is worth to open that door,' he said. Prendergast leaned over the desk. 'Even if I wanted to, I don't have the key,' said Evans, his voice taking on a squeaky quality. His hands remained affixed to the edge of the desk, but he was now leaning backwards away from Prendergast.

'Why, you little whippersnapper,' he said in a low menacing voice, 'if you don't open that door at once I will use your head as a battering ram.'

I stepped forward. 'I hardly think that would be appropriate,' I said sternly.

Prendergast turned around. Evans finally released his hold and bolted into the backroom, shutting the door behind him. Not, I thought, a man of great moral fibre.

'I will thank you not to interfere, ma'am. This is a Gentlemen's Club.'

'Then I suggest you start behaving like one,' I said. 'I can confirm that Mr Stapleford is acting on orders from the Foreign Office. I believe officials are currently on the way here. I am sure when they arrive everything will be explained to your satisfaction.' I stood my ground, but I felt nervous. Although, moments before, he had appeared the gentleman, Prendergast's colour was up and his eyes glistened in a most unpleasant way. I did not think he was fully in control of himself.

He pointed his cane at me. 'Poppycock,' he said. 'I do not believe for one moment that a woman would be more au fait with events than myself. If there was a serious situation in the club I would have been informed. I am the honorary secretary.'

'Perhaps Mr Stapleford is unaware of your position,' I said. 'You do not appear to be wearing a badge.'

I had gone too far. The man raised his cane. I cut in at once. 'I suggest you think very carefully about your next action. I am the granddaughter of an Earl. My fiancé is also present. Neither would take kindly to you behaving in such an ungentlemanly manner.'

Prendergast uttered what can only be described as a growl and stalked off. Richenda, who had not left my side, emitted a loud breath. 'Well done,' she said. 'I thought he was going to go for us there. Nasty piece of work.'

'Isn't he just,' I said. 'And if it proves that Lovelock

73

was murdered I would put him top of my list of suspects.'

'Oh,' said Richenda. 'Are you about to have another adventure? Only, I do not think your mother will approve. And is Bertram really working for the Foreign Office? I know he speaks French, but I've never thought of him as the type to take charge in a situation.'

I shook my head. 'We should go and find him,' I said. 'He can explain better than I.'

'He's gone now,' I called over the desk. Evans' head appeared round the side of the door jamb, quickly followed by his body. He was holding an umbrella. 'I went to get this to defend you, ladies,' he said quite unable to look either of us in the eye. 'I'm not up to much with my fists, so I got a weapon.'

'How thoughtful,' said Richenda. 'It doesn't matter now. My friend has seen him off with her best weapon - British grit and a sterling backbone.'

Evans had the grace to blush. I noticed, however, that he placed the umbrella under the counter in easy reach. 'Is Mr Prendergast often so - so irate?' I asked him.

'Not often, miss. He had a bad time in Africa. Apparently, before he went out there he was known as a jovial personage at the club.'

'That would be why they elected him secretary,' said Richenda.

Evans nodded and opened his eyes wide enough to show their whites all the way round. 'I hear terrible things happened to him in the jungle.'

'Oh, do tell,' said Richenda promptly.

'I couldn't,' said Evans. 'Even thinking about them tales gives me the heebie-jeebies.'

'Was he a friend of Mr Lovelock?' I asked and then quickly added. 'I wondered if his demise might have unsettled him.'

'Not that I know of, Miss. They were of different generations, if you ask me.'

I thanked him and tipped him a shilling. 'You will have earned yourself a pint in the local establishment by the end of the day,' I said. He gave me an odd look, but swiftly pocketed the shilling.

As we walked away Richenda said, 'It is not really the role of a lady to tip.' She blushed slightly. 'Not that I am saying I know how to be a lady better than you do.'

'I would not do so normally, but Bertram never carries pocket change. Rory McLeod saw to all that sort of thing. It seems unfair that such gratuities should go undistributed because your brother cannot carry change without fiddling in his trouser pockets in a most unseemly manner.' Richenda suppressed a laugh and only succeeded in snorting.

We found Bertram on his own in the corridor. He was pacing back and forth, clearly deep in thought. 'Has the man with the tools still not appeared?' I asked.

Bertram looked up and blinked owlishly. 'What? Yes. Been and gone. Work of a moment to get into the drawer. Useless lock. Remind me to get McLeod to check the locks at White Orchards.' Then he remembered and looked particularly glum. 'I suppose I shall have to do it,' he said and sighed as if he had given himself a Herculean task. He began to pace once more.

'Were the papers there?' I asked.

'What? No. Empty as a poor man's purse,' said Bertram. 'I've locked us all in.'

'I do hope you haven't swallowed the keys,' said Richenda. 'He did that once, you know, when we were small. Locked Richard in a wardrobe and swallowed the key.'

'Of course I haven't swallowed the keys. They are in a secure place.'

'Good,' I said. 'There are some difficult people here.' And I told him of our encounter with Prendergast.

'What a rotter!' said Bertram. 'Not that you didn't send him on his way with a flea in his ear. Jolly good show and all that. Thing is, I've a whole smoking room full of the fellows and I'm rather concerned that Fitzroy would want me to take matters forward. I've told the waiting staff and the porters they must stay too, but no one seems to be able to find me a duty sheet, so I can't be sure no one slipped away.'

'Surely you don't think a waiter stole these papers?' said Richenda. 'Or was the man murdered?'

'No, and I don't know,' said Bertram.

Richenda looked to me for explanation. 'What Bertram is thinking is that, although it is most unlikely that one of the staff stole the papers, it is quite possible that one of them might be persuaded - with a suitable economic endorsement - to smuggle the papers out.'

'Oh, I see,' said Richenda. 'How clever of you to think of that.'

'As for the unexplained death, we have learnt that Lovelock often took heroin, having been prescribed it many years ago. It is an old habit of his, but it is always possible that he accidentally overdosed. It may be like some other medicines in that one can build up a tolerance to it. Do you know about such things, Bertram?' I asked.

'Dammit, Euphemia! I wanted to keep the sordid parts from you. How did you... don't tell me, Fitzroy.'

'He called again to say he is being detained even longer than he hoped.'

'Rats,' said Bertram. 'We will have to interview them, then. That is, if you will help, Euphemia. I think a woman's touch might keep things calmer.'

'Or infuriate them,' said Richenda. 'I don't think you should tell Euphemia's mother and stepfather that you work for the Foreign Office.'

'We don't,' said Bertram.

'Then explain your situation to me,' said Richenda.

Bertram and I looked helplessly at each other.

'Perhaps I should ask this Fitzroy when he appears.'

'I wouldn't do that,' said Bertram anxiously. 'He's a tricky fellow. You don't want anything to do with him. I don't want anything to do with him.' The latter part of the speech was said with deep feeling.

'Well, for now, I shall leave you and Euphemia to do whatever it is you are not doing and return to the lounge. I assume everyone there can be ruled out as they would have been in eyeshot while Mr Lovelock died? Or was he quite cold when you found him?'

'Poor fellow was still warm,' said Bertram and gave a small shudder.

'I believe it takes a certain amount of time for the living warmth to leave a body,' Richenda remarked. 'I read about it in the Mystical Section of *Country Hostess*. Your friend Madame Arcana writes the column.'

'Go away,' said Bertram. 'Not you, Euphemia, you need to come and meet the members I've managed to round up. They're all in the smoking room.'

'Will there be drinks?' said Richenda.

We both looked blankly at her.

'During the introductions? Is there anyone interesting amongst them?'

'It's not that kind of introduction, Richenda,' I said

77

quickly before Bertram responded in a blistering manner. Richenda was far from unintelligent, but she defaulted to a society frame of mind rather than a murder investigation one. Something that had become the reverse for Bertram and me. 'We will be asking them questions to ascertain if any of them have accidentally removed -'

'Or stolen,' said Bertram.

'The memoirs of Mr Lovelock.'

'Or even killed him for them,' said Bertram.

'Golly!' said Richenda. 'What on earth do you ask that makes people confess?'

'If only it were that easy,' I said. 'It's usually more about working out why someone would want to do - well, whatever has been done.'

'I don't know, Euphemia, we have had one or two notable confessions,' said Bertram, giving me a wink. He seemed to be cheering up now there was actual work to do. Or, perhaps, he liked looking more knowledgeable than his older sister.

'Is it interesting?' asked Richenda.

I shifted position quickly, treading on Bertram's foot before he answered.

'Ouch,' said Bertram, regarding me like a puppy who had been kicked.

'No,' I said. 'It's very boring.'

'Oh, well, maybe I should help,' said Richenda, sounding a lot less keen. 'I don't want to shirk my responsibilities.'

'I think you might be too intimidating,' I said quickly. 'Why don't we bring you in later?'

'As a sort of specialist?' said Richenda.

Bertram glowered at me and rubbed his foot.

I was suddenly struck by an idea. 'Actually, what you

could do is take a look around the place. If Bertram has the main suspects corralled in the smoking lounge, and my family is in the coffee lounge, you could take a look about the place. I doubt the porters will like it, but there's not a lot they can say if you say you're helping Bertram.'

'You mean I can say I'm with the Foreign Office?' said Richenda, her voice rising to an excited squeak.

'No,' I said. 'Bertram doesn't work for the Foreign Office. He has received a request from them and you are aiding him. It's not the same thing.'

Richenda tossed her head in a remarkably excellent impression of her favourite horse. 'You're splitting hairs.'

'No, she's not -' began Bertram.

I interrupted him again. 'Believe me, Richenda, you would not like to face down the people who are on the way and explain why you are impersonating government officials. Technically, I believe they could still throw you in the Tower. The Tower of London,' I added when she frowned.

'Think how the children would miss you if you were incarcerated anywhere,' added Bertram in a master stroke.

'All right,' said Richenda. 'I have been wondering what is upstairs.' She headed off down the corridor.

'Do you think we should tell her to be careful?' I said.

'I think we should tell the staff to hide,' said Bertram frankly. He scowled at me. 'I do wish you would stop stepping on my feet. It's become quite a habit. I never realised you were so clumsy.'

'I'm not,' I said. 'But I will keep you from trying to say inappropriate things.'

Bertram's scowl deepened. 'I suppose being an honourable you would know.'

'So, who am to meet?' I asked, refusing to take the bait.

'It is easier to show.' He gave a great sigh. 'Do not expect them to like you.'

As we walked along the red carpeted corridor together I said, 'It was most clever of you to lock the doors. Where did you put the key?'

'If you don't know they can't force it out of you,' said Bertram grimly.

I did my best to suppress a smile but failed. 'It is only a group of older gentlemen in the smoking room, is it not? Short of waving their canes at us, what can they do?'

'Explain that to Lovelock,' said Bertram and threw open the smoking room door.

Chapter Eight
In Which I Behave in a Most Ladylike Way and am also Quite Undignified

The moment the door opened my eyes began to water. I have heard others talk of the fog of a smoking room, but at all the houses where I have been, and gained admittance to this sacred male arena, there had never been that many smokers. The same could not be said here. Tendrils of smoke reached out towards me and the extremely strong odour of cigars assaulted my nostrils.

'Rather slaps one in the face, doesn't it.' said Bertram, giving a slight cough.

I waved my hand in front me. 'How utterly ridiculous,' I said, sounding and feeling like my mother. I strode into the mists. I managed to collide only with two small tables, before I staggered to the other side of the room and threw open a window. The cries of alarm and anger that greeted this action could surely have been no more than if I had thrown a bomb into the place. Indeed, they might have preferred a bomb, as it would have added to both the smoke and fog.

The smoke fled with surprising alacrity out of the sash window I had thrown up. I had feared it might be nailed shut, but it opened with an ease that suggested that sometimes, when the room was empty, the staff must come and air the room. For this I could only be grateful. The tobacco smell, one I normally do not mind, was enough to make a cat sick. Shelves of books lined the room, but I doubt they were ever read. On the walls above the bookcases that rose only two-thirds of the way up the wall were the stuffed heads of a number of tropical animals. All of these were portrayed bearing their fangs as testament to the brave hunters who brought them down. The room was littered with chairs, both wing-backed and chesterfield, a number of small tables, and a single larger one. On these tables was a variety of humidors, ashtrays, decanters, half-full glasses of spirits, and soda siphons. In the corner stood a small unit filled with what appeared to be packs of cards, game boards, and boxes of pieces. The overall effect was to give the room a cluttered and crowded appearance. The windows, of which there were two, were along one side of the room, and faced out of the back of the building into the gardens beyond. Though the lawns were neat there appeared to be no sign of activity outside. I could imagine that at the height of summer it would be perfect for cricket or croquet, but I was yet to see evidence of enough active members to make up a half-decent team. The door and the fireplace faced each other. The impressive marble hearth had been stacked up with logs upon logs. Next to it sat a large basket of more fresh logs, and close to this, practically in the hearth itself, sat the irascible gentleman Richenda and I had previously met, Prendergast.

'It's a damn woman!' As the air cleared I saw that the cry had come from a gentleman with impressive grey mutton chops, which he had presumably cultivated to distract the onlooker from his balding pate. However, what drew my attention was the upturned table and cards lying on the floor.

'Oh, I am sorry,' I said. 'Did I ruin your game?'

The gentleman in question seemed only to notice the upturned table at that very moment. 'Garr!' he cried showing off hideously brown-stained teeth. 'Garr! Damn ruddy woman! That game was finally working out for me! I've been playing since Friday and was in line to beat Cole-Sutton's record. Porter! Porter! There's a bloody woman in here. Throw her out, I say. Throw her out.'

Of course, no porter responded to his cries as they had been forewarned of our entrance.

'Chapelford, mind your manners,' said an older gentleman with snowy white hair. He was seated in a wingback chair opposite a much younger blond gentleman. 'As you can see, our chess board also took a tumble. And I do believe young Davenport was about to beat me for the very first time!'

'I don't know about that, sir,' said Davenport. 'But I put up a good show for sure,' he said this with a nervous laugh.

'Don't know what you're all complaining about,' said a red-haired middle-aged gentleman, who was sitting closer to one of the windows and as far as possible from the stoked up fire. 'I'm always saying we need more fresh air in here. Good for the lungs, don't you know?' He thumped his chest. 'Never had a cough in my life. Put it down to my outdoor life. Mind you, Prendergast will probably expire in the next few minutes. Wants it as hot as damned Africa, don't you know! Ha! Ha!'

As the other members in the room averted their eyes from him in a unanimous show of embarrassment, Prendergast stared into the fire. 'These are the supposed pair from the foreign office I told you about. They have us locked in.' His head jerked and he glowered at Bertram. 'Are they going to compensate me for my deal going south? If I don't make the meeting for four o'clock,' he produced a half-hunter from his waistcoat pocket, 'I will lose thousands. Possibly tens of thousands. What do you say about that, damn you? You jumped-up civil servant. You give these people an iota of power and they take advantage of their betters whenever they can. And as for the woman the *honourable* woman – since when did our government start employing females in positions of authority?'

'I do not believe I have said at any time that I am a civil servant,' said Bertram, loudly and with a great deal of dignity. 'I merely said that I had orders from the Foreign Office. As for the lady, she is my fiancée, and I demand you apologise for your boorish behaviour at once.'

'If the lady wishes to be treated as such then I suggest she comports herself like one,' said Prendergast.

Bertram's face went very red. Before I could stop him, he strode across the room, ending up mere inches from Prendergast's chair. 'Stand up,' he demanded. 'Stand up this moment, sir!'

'Why? So you can try and knock me down again?' said Prendergast. 'I have no appetite to be made sport of, sir.'

I breathed a sigh of relief. It was clear to all the fellow was a coward. Now all that remained was for Bertram to retreat with dignity. I should have known that retreat was not a word in Bertram's dictionary of acceptable gentlemanly actions. He turned to the nearest table, picked up a soda siphon, and with a swiftness no one foresaw, squirted at Prendergast. The fresh air enthusiast burst into laughter at the sight of Prendergast with soda water dripping down his face and onto his immaculate shirt and waistcoat. But from the others in the room, their reaction was a combined intake of breath that boded ill for Bertram. The man himself seemed a bit surprised by the effectiveness of the siphon, and put it back on the table beside him, before taking a step back and raising his fists.

With deliberate slowness, Prendergast took a handkerchief from his top pocket and wiped his face as best he could. Then he threw it on the fire where it went up with a sudden hiss. Leaning on his cane he pulled himself up to his full height. 'How dare you,' he said in a quiet voice that dripped menace. 'Do you know who I am?'

'You are the man who insulted my fiancée,' said Bertram. I felt both enormously proud of him and frightened out of my wits at the same time. Prendergast towered above him by easily ten inches. His suit was well cut and showed a lean frame; as to whether that was also a muscled frame I could not ascertain. I only knew that Bertram was rarely physically active and had close to his sister's famed fondness for pudding. I also knew that strenuous exercise would undoubtedly bring on his heart condition, making him ill, or worse. I could feel the blood rushing away from my face as I contemplated Bertram once again lying immobile on the floor before me. I turned towards the door but felt myself sway slightly. I caught the end of a shelf to steady myself. This was no time for swooning.[14] I felt sweat break out on my forehead. My stomach churned. I could face many dangers, but the thought of the loss of Bertram - I could not endure it. I had to go and get help, but the room had begun to swim around me. Darkness circled the edge of my vision. I heard a voice from a long way away say, 'Look to the lady,' before my senses deserted me.

I awoke to the aggressively paisley-patterned ladies

---

[14]An occupational hazard that, before embarking on this lifestyle, I had believed to be no more than a feminine attempt for attention.

powder room. I lay on my side and directly opposite me in one of the armchairs sat Bertram, pale featured and with an expression of concern on his face, but most definitely alive. I heaved a sigh of relief. Bertram immediately stood and came over to me. 'How do you feel?' he asked. 'Is your head sore? No one could be sure if you hit your head when you fell.'

I raised my head experimentally off the cushion and my vision swam. I lowered it back down. 'I rather think I must have,' I said. 'My head does not hurt, but I feel dizzy.' Bertram squatted beside my chaise longue and turned his head sideways to look at me straight on.

'Oh, my Lord! Oh, my days! To think the Holby Club has come to this! And under my watch?' cried a male voice.

I flinched slightly. 'I thought we were alone.'

'That's Gilbert Parry,' said Bertram. 'He's the head steward. Davenport, the young gentleman, ran to get him when Mr Wilkes drew our attention to your fainting.'

'Wilkes?'

'Sebastian Wilkes, old chap with the monocle. He called Prendergast and me to order.' I saw a faint blush on Bertram's cheeks.

'It was a terribly stupid thing to do,' I said. 'And I am terribly proud of you.'

Bertram's blush deepened. 'Why the devil did you faint? It's not the kind of behaviour I am used to seeing from you. Is it anything to do with being - you know - who you really are again?'

At this point I sat up, ignoring the slight double vision that overlaid the room as much as I could. The paisley really was frightful. I could now also see Gilbert Parry, a middle-aged man slightly going to seed, dressed in the typical Holby outfit that the other stewards and porters wore, but with a large gold-crested badge on his waistcoat. I couldn't see what it said. My eyes were drawn to the paisley tie he wore. What I had assumed to be an accidental interior decoration disaster turned out to be a motif of the club. That this fascinated me gave me an inkling that all was not yet right in my head.

Bertram stood up and rubbed his neck. 'Thank goodness. I much prefer you the right way up. I was getting a terrible crick in my neck.'

'Why is he here?' I asked.

'He's chaperoning me - I think. Gentlemen aren't allowed in the Ladies' area. Things no man should see and all that.'

'The whole Club is going to rack and ruin,' said Parry.

'I would much prefer it if you would leave us alone,' I said. 'Mr Stapleford is my fiancée.'

'Can't do, ma'am,' he said in the tone of an official who dearly loved his position.

I let it go. 'What did you just say to me?' I asked Bertram.

'Oh nothing,' said Bertram. 'You might care to know that engaging in fisticuffs is not allowed within the club boundaries, so Prendergast wouldn't have touched me.'

'He's the honorary secretary,' I said. I began to gingerly probe my cranial dome with my fingers. Nothing felt obviously soft or squishy. 'Could I get some water, please?'

'Wouldn't brandy be better?' asked Bertram.

'Only if you want me to be sick,' I said.

Parry moaned aloud at the thought.

'You heard the lady,' said Bertram. 'I can't go and get it. I have no idea where to find it. Besides, I'm not a member anyway.'

'Not a member?' said Parry. He sniffed haughtily and left.

Bertram offered me his arm. 'Not entirely sure that bloke is coming back. Good riddance, I say. But I think I should escort you through to the coffee lounge. Bound to be decent beverages there. Can you walk?'

'I'd really rather not,' I said.

Bertram looked nonplussed for a moment. 'Oh, your mother. Kept her out of it so far. Club very keen on hushing everything up. Why, I think they'd mail poor Lovelock's body to the cemetery if they thought the Post Office would collect.'

I gave a faint smile and stood up. My vision had regained its single focus and if my legs felt a little shaky I only had to apply a small amount of my weight on Bertram's arm to steady myself.

'That's a girl,' said Bertram approvingly. 'Why don't we go through to the little interviewing room Parry has set up. You won't want to miss any of that, will you?' He coughed lightly. 'Don't suppose you feel up to taking the notes, do you? Only my handwriting is pretty dire.'

'I am certain the gentlemen will be much less concerned about my presence if they think I am fulfilling secretarial duties,' I said.

'Oh, jolly good thought,' said Bertram in the fake tones of someone trying to force an idea. I gave him a wry smile. He looked contrite. 'It is better if they think you are my support staff,' he said. 'Sorry.'

I shook my head and immediately regretted it. I let go of Bertram's arm and lurched into the facilities area. I made it in time. To give him his due, Bertram stayed his ground and shouted encouraging phrases through to me like, 'Better out than in, old girl,' and, 'I always feel a lot better when I've had a good vomit.' As I rested my head against the cold china I wished he would stop being cheerful and more than anything that he would go away. Finally, I could take it no more.

'Please, Bertram,' I called. 'Go and fetch my mother.'

Chapter Nine
Interviews Begin

Cold compresses, iced soda, lavender water, and ginger biscuits did their work. Only my mother could have whipped the Holby staff into shape. Of course, she vocally disapproved of me at length, but she kept her voice soft and gradually the headache brought on by my sickness began to fade. I think she would also have sent for a doctor, but Bertram came back and blundered around for a while. My mother got rid of him with ease, but he returned with The Bishop. Giles Hawthorn, it proved, was more than a match for my mother, so that instead of lying resting on the chaise until Fitzroy and his men arrived, I found myself sitting in a small chamber behind a desk with a fresh notepad and pencil in front of me. Bertram sat alongside me. 'Sorry, Euphemia, but I know what that rotter will say if we don't do this by the book.'

I sighed and objected for the hundredth time that we were not police.

'We are agents of the Crown, who have been called to investigate the unexplained death of Killian Lovelock,' said Bertram. 'As such we have more power than the police.'

'Did that man tell you to say that?'

'He said to say it only if I really found myself in a corner,' said Bertram. 'I haven't had to pull the big guns on anyone yet - save you.'

'My mother,' I said.

'No, your step-pa did that. Damn me, if I don't think

she liked having the reins taken out of her hands. She complained like anything, but I'm pretty clear I saw the glint of respect in her eyes.'

I turned my head slowly towards him. 'I am nothing like my mother,' I said, and saw the upstart spark of hope in his eyes die. 'So, who is first?'

'I thought we'd start with the easy one,' said Bertram. 'The old chap. Parry is about to send him in.'

Even as he spoke the door opened and Gilbert Parry announced, as if it was a royal drawing room, 'Mr Sebastian Wilkes.'

Mr Wilkes came forward. He took Bertram's outstretched hand and shook it. Then to my surprise he took my hand and bowed over it. 'I hope you are much recovered, my dear. A nasty little scene for you to witness.' For a moment I thought he was speaking of Lovelock's body, but then I realised. 'Thank you, I am feeling much better,' I said.

Wilkes sat down in the chair opposite, spreading out his jacket carefully. 'It quite warmed my heart to see such an act of chivalry in these modern times.' He pronounced 'modern' with extreme distaste. 'Even if it was a little ill-advised,' he added with a tip of his head to Bertram.

'Yes, well,' spluttered my fiancé, who was unsure if he was being complimented or chastised. 'All done for now. Better get on to the business at hand. Can you give us your full name, please, sir?'

Wilkes smiled. 'How very like a police interview! Very well, I am Sebastian Walter Henry Wilkes. I am a publisher of magazines and newspapers. I have recently also begun my first imprint. It will feature crime novels. It may be of interest to you.' The latter part of the speech was aimed at me.

I wrote down what he said. 'And what do you do?' said Bertram, who had set himself a determined course. 'What? No!' he said. 'You have already answered that. How did you know Killian Lovelock?'

'I didn't, really,' said Wilkes. 'Of course, I saw him around at the club. It's been the cause of some mirth that he's been writing his memoirs. We all knew what he was actually doing in that room. Everyday. Quite excessive. It's all very sad, but not unexpected.'

'Doing?' I queried.

Wilkes raised an eyebrow. 'Daydreaming,' he said. 'Let's put it like that.'

'You mean injecting himself with heroin,' I said. 'I agree it is not a savoury habit, but as far as I am aware it is not illegal. Many doctors prescribe it. I believe patients prefer it to other medication as it makes them feel heroic. Hence the name.' There, I thought, that will show him I am not some ignorant feminine fainter.

'Indeed,' said Wilkes, without either a change of tone or expression. 'The unsavoury part comes when the originating disease has fled, but the patient continues to inject because of the feelings the drug inspires. Over time a man will find he requires more and more of such a drug to attain such feelings and, so I am told, he is never able to regain quite that perfect euphoria he experienced on first use. It is particularly sad in older men - the drug allows them to recapture their feelings of youth for a short while. I feel that it is what Lovelock was doing.'

'Are you suggesting there never were any memoirs?' I asked.

'Very acute,' said Wilkes. A momentary thought struck me, but it was gone before I could capture it. 'No, I do not believe the memoirs ever existed. I believe it was an excuse. I certainly never saw any sign of them. Besides, I am unsure what exactly Lovelock would have had to write about. He spent his life in clerical obscurity as a civil servant, from what I know. Not that I know a great deal. I have been searching my memories since you asked to see me, and I cannot honestly say the fellow made much of an impression on me.' He shrugged. 'I do not wish to speak ill of the dead, but I know neither anything good or bad about Killian Lovelock. As far as I am concerned, he lived, he died. There was no story in between.'

'That is sad,' I said. 'He leaves no family?'

'I could not tell you. One of the other members, or Parry, may know. Lovelock and I rarely spoke. If we did it would be to remark on the weather or pass the decanter across the room. Nothing more.'

'I would have thought with you being in the publishing industry, and him writing his memoirs, he would have been eager to talk to you,' said Bertram. 'To procure some kind of a deal or whatever it is authors do.'

Wilkes laughed. 'Ah, I have misled you. I own some newspapers, and I am soon to own a small publishing house, but I let those who know how to do things run the business. I am very much - what would you say - a sleeping partner.'

'Some might consider that an odd choice,' I said. 'If you have no interest in the newspaper medium. After all, it has considerable influence on the population. An owner might choose to encourage his editors to lean one way or another to influence popular taste.'

'As in which hosiery to buy?' said Wilkes. 'I am not interested in influencing the general market. People are well able to choose their footwear without my assistance.'

'I meant,' I said, laying down my pencil to study his

features, 'that one might influence general opinion on matters such as whether a war with Germany will be good or bad for this country.'

Wilkes' eyes narrowed, though otherwise his expression didn't change. He didn't reach for his monocle, but he studied me for slightly longer than was polite or comfortable before he answered. 'It will be bad for those fighting and good for those selling arms,' he said. 'That much is obvious. I trust the British public to realise such a thing without my help and also, of course, his Majesty, whose subjects we have the honour to be.' At this point he stood up and bowing to us both said, 'I believe we are finished here.'

'Ah, yes, for now,' Bertram said, trying to take control. Wilkes exited, and Bertram sat down. He took out his handkerchief and mopped his head. 'Not too bad, hmm?' he said. 'Did you get the notes down?' As I was still scribbling at this stage I didn't answer immediately. 'Odd chap, reminds me of someone,' said Bertram.

'Who is Parry sending in next?' I asked, finally laying down my pencil.

'I wish it was brandy,' said Bertram. 'I'll never be hard on a police inspector again. They have the rottenest jobs. I mean, we're one of them, and look how they are treating us!'

The door opened, 'Mr Gordon Chapelford,' announced Parry.

'Good Gad! That female is still here!' This was uttered in a sort of klaxon cry, but when the steward simply shut the door behind him instead of forcibly removing me, Chapelford sat down. He gave no pretence at politeness. He clearly disapproved of us. 'What's this all about then?' he said.

'So, what do you do?' said Bertram.

'I am a chartered accountant to the great and good of this land. Who, might I ask, are you?'

'An agent of the Crown,' said Bertram.

'And what pray is an agent of the Crown doing in The Holby Club. It's not like this a is top-drawer establishment. After all, the buggers let me in.' I felt the blood rush to my face. Quickly, I looked down at my notepad, but I was too late. 'That's why we shouldn't let females in here. Too ruddy delicate,' said Chapelford.

Bertram shuffled some papers, which I knew were blank. Clearly, the manner in which the gentlemen were entering did not fit with the script he had prepared, and it was throwing him. I kept my tongue behind my teeth. I knew I would be doing Bertram no favours if I interjected in this interview. Wilkes, I had sensed, had no intrinsic objection to women. He had acknowledged me politely on entrance, the very opposite of this heathen.

'What was your relationship with Killian Lovelock?' said Bertram.

'I didn't have a bloody relationship,' said Chapelford. 'Barely knew the man. I come here to eat a good dinner and have a decent smoke. Not interested in any chitter-chatter. Plenty of that at home, ha!'

I looked up through my eyelashes and considered the man. Gravy stains on his clothing, teeth rotting in his mouth, and the hair on his head resembling some form of chronic mange – if he had a wife, as he implied, I truly pitied the woman. That a woman should be in thrall to such a vile creature as this brought forth all my suffragette sympathies. But, however loathsome he might be as an individual, I knew that did not make him a murderer. I waited impatiently for Bertram to ask his next question.

However, he seemed quite as taken aback as me to think this man had a mate.

'You're married?' he blurted out.

'Yes, what's it to you?'

'Do you spend a lot of time at the Holby?' said Bertram.

'I just told you I'm married.' He gave a hoarse braying laugh. 'Of course I ruddy well do. Why would I want to be at home with all those brats whining?'

Dear God, it was worse. He'd not only married, but he had bred. I felt my gorge rising. Those poor children.

'Would I know your wife?' I asked as calmly as I could.

'Doubt it,' said Chapelford. 'Expect we move in different circles, besides, you're what, twenty-four? She is nineteen. Married me at sixteen and a half.'

Neither Bertram nor I could find the words.

'That it?' said Chapelford. 'Waste of bleeding time.'

He had half risen before Bertram managed to say, 'Lovelock's memoirs, did you ever see them?'

'What? That pile of papers that he carried around with him? Yes, I saw them. Never read any of them. More interested in figures. Of both kinds,' he said with a sneer at me.

When he had gone, Bertram said, 'Did he want us to hate him?' He was mopping his head with handkerchief again.

'He was the very character of loathsomeness,' I said.

'More like a caricature of himself than a real person,' said Bertram thoughtfully. 'I don't think we should believe a word he says.'

'Even about the memoirs?' I said.

Bertram shook his head. 'I know these gentlemen are

trying for their own amusement to make my life as difficult as possible, but Chapelford said what everyone one might expect of him. I'd like to think I was a fine judge of character, but honestly, Amy could have predicted every word that came out of his mouth.'

'I hope not!'

Bertram laughed. 'Well, not every word. But something along the lines of scruffy, smelly, rude, bad man.'

'Pretty much. How on earth do you think he convinced that girl to marry him?'

'If it's true - and I say if - I imagine it was some kind of business arrangement. Someone needed him to sort out the books and he needed a wife. He's fifty if he's a day. I think we rule out a love match.'

'Good Lord, yes,' I said. I sighed. 'Maybe he shows a different side of himself to his wife.'

'I hope it's a cleaner side anyway,' said Bertram. 'We've another three to go. Do you fancy a cup of tea? I could do with a break.' He held up his damp handkerchief. 'And a new handkerchief.'

Chapter Ten
Bertram and I Do Our Best to Recover

'We don't know if Lovelock was writing on paper or in a notebook,' I said, dropping my third lump of sugar in my tea. Parry was keeping the hordes away while we sat in the little chamber and drank our tea. Neither of us wanted to run into members of our respective families.

Bertram glanced up. He had half a macaroon in his mouth. He crunched it hurriedly and then swept the crumbs off his waistcoat. 'You won't let me turn into a Chapelford, will you?' he said.

I shook my head. 'I would shoot you first.'

'Very comforting,' said Bertram. 'I can believe it. Try and get Fitzroy to teach you to aim straight if you do.'

'You mean keep it painless, like people do for old dogs?'

'You'd shoot a dog?' said Bertram, horrified.

'Of course not,' I said.

'But you'd shoot me?'

'That's different,' I said.

Bertram gave me a defiant glare and reached for a second macaroon. 'I see what you mean. We don't know if we can trust Chapelford. Saying he saw papers might have been no more than a guess.'

'I can't see why he would want to throw us off the scent.'

'He wants us out of the club,' said Bertram miserably. 'Probably thinks any kind of scandal that comes near him will affect business.'

'Especially if you were right and he did amend someone's accounts for them,' I said and took a sip of tea.

'Hang on, Euphemia! We were joking around. I didn't accuse the chap of being dodgy.'

'But suppose you were right, and he does arrange financial affairs for people. You know, making it look like they have slightly more money than they do, to get a loan or some such thing.' I sighed. 'I admit I don't know much about that world, but there are occasions when people - and businesses - want their accounts to appear different to how they are.'

'Yes,' said Bertram. 'Never wanted to go into the family bank, but Father made me learn about it all the same. So, yes, accountants that can hide transactions and that kind of thing are highly sought after by a few.'

'It's illegal?'

'Oh, yes,' said Bertram. 'If you're caught in a fraud of some kind then you're liable to lose not only your liberty, but your possessions and your reputation.'

'So, the last thing he wants is anyone investigating people here,' I said. 'I'm betting he sought membership of the club to find the right contacts.'

Bertram shook his head. 'I think it's more likely his contacts got him in. I mean, look at the man, who'd vote to admit him.'

'I agree, when you stand him alongside Prendergast or Wilkes he looks like a tramp,' I said.

'I think we are agreed we can discount most of what he says,' said Bertram. 'He's trying to get us away from here for various nefarious reasons and so he will object, obscure, and, as a last ditch, agree with anything we say as long as it makes us leave. Phew. How would Fitzroy deal with a character like that?'

I bit into a small fancy iced cake. 'Probably torture,' I said through a mouthful of delightfully light and moist sponge.

Bertram's eyebrows rose in alarm. 'Did you ever think you would condone such a thing while eating cake?' he demanded.

'I never said I condoned it,' I said. 'But I suppose I am capable of considering things a little more cold-bloodedly than when I first met you. Mind you, the first thing Richenda ever asked of me was to help her move a corpse.'

Bertram leant a little nearer to me. 'I've been thinking, Euphemia, when we're married, don't you think it might be an idea to leave all this stuff behind?'

'What stuff in particular?' I asked warily. I knew we would have to spend much of our time in the Fens at White Orchards, but I had hoped that the occasional London visit was not out of the question.

'Fitzroy, murder, spies, assassins and all that.'

'Oh, that,' I said. 'Yes, if you wish. We've done more than our bit for the country. Much more than most private citizens.'

Bertram nodded eagerly. 'Yes, time to let someone else have all the fun.'

I smiled at him. 'Some of it has been fun, and it let us find each other.'

Bertram reached over and laid his hand over mine. 'Only reason I will never regret it,' he said.

'Mind you, it's all very well deciding what we want to do,' I said. 'Fitzroy is the one we will have to convince.'

'Does that mean we should do this investigation well or badly?' said Bertram.

'Bertram! We will, as ever, do our best to see that

justice is done.'

'Yes, Euphemia,' said Bertram sadly. 'I expect we had better get back to it.'

I flicked through my notes on the pad. 'There were a couple of things I noticed,' I said. 'Prendergast, we know, has a violent temper, and made it clear earlier that he disliked civil servants.'

Bertram's eyes lit up. 'And Wilkes said Lovelock was some kind of civil servant. Normally I'd say that wasn't sufficient grounds to murder someone, but that chap has a short fuse if what he did, or at least tried to do, to the porter is anything to go by.'

'But he didn't take up your challenge,' I said. 'Do you think he is the type of man who only berates his inferiors?'

'Yellow-bellied, you mean,' said Bertram. 'But then there is that club rule about members not brawling on the premises. He might be the sort that lives for those sorts of rules. From what I can gather, being an Hon Sec is a mightily dull and tiresome task. Lots of lists of names and writing down what was said at meetings that everyone says is wrong afterwards and then contests.' His brows lowered.

'Could it be you were Secretary for a club at school?' I asked.

'Three clubs,' said Bertram. 'Worst year of my life. I mean, you think you know a chap and then you report what he says ever so slightly wrong and the rotter rats you out to the beak at every opportunity.'

I didn't bother to ask what he meant; the day was wearing on. 'So, he would refrain from attacking a fellow member, though not a porter,' I said. 'That still doesn't sound like the kind of man who would break the law, least of all for the serious crime of murder.'

'I see your point,' said Bertram. 'But we can't discount his temper.'

'Apparently something happened to him in Africa,' I said. 'I've heard people hint at it, but no one will say - or no one knows - what caused his volatile temperament.'

'I say,' said Bertram. 'If he was cool as a cucumber before he went out, and now he's a raging rhinoceros, then that's a jolly good case for mental instability. Which would make him a fine contender for being our murderer.'

'Raging rhinoceros?'

'Alliteration, for effect,' said Bertram. 'Only this minute remembered it. Must have been that talking about school that did it.' He shivered slightly.

'But the thing is,' I said, 'we don't know if it was murder or if Lovelock simply took too much heroin. We don't even know if the memoirs were real.'

'Pretty much back where we started,' said Bertram.

'I would be inclined to say that it is all a storm in a tea-cup. But...'

'But?'

'Well, when you spoke to Fitzroy did he seem odd to you?'

'He always seems odd to me,' said Bertram. 'But I get what you mean. He was rather stern.'

'Really? He was quite kind to me.'

Bertram uttered a noise that can only be described as a growling grunt.

'What was he stern about with you?'

'Finding the memoirs.'

'So, he definitely believes they existed? He didn't say if they'd never existed or anything like that?'

Bertram paused to think and ate another macaroon. 'No, he didn't infer they weren't real.'

'Well, that's odd. If this fellow was nothing but a minor civil servant all this life.'

Bertram fiddled with a lump of sugar. 'Would you call what Fitzroy does being a civil servant?'

'I suppose you could,' I said. 'He always claims he works for the Crown. Oh, are you suggesting that Lovelock was another Fitzroy?'

'I imagine Fitzroy's memoirs would be rather -'

'Spectacular,' I finished.

'I was going to say embarrassing,' said Bertram. 'To lots of people in high places. That man brims with other people's secrets.'

'If only I'd got a better look at the body,' I said. Bertram started. 'Well, you know how Fitzroy keeps himself in excellent shape...' I continued.

'I hadn't noticed,' said Bertram in surprisingly cold tones.

'A lot of what he does is physical, I believe.'

'I couldn't say,' said Bertram.

'I imagine it becomes a habit, so I would think it likely that Lovelock would have kept himself in good shape despite his age - or for his age. I mean we don't even know if he was in active service.'

'You know all the language, don't you?' said Bertram.

'I've picked it up as we've gone along,' I said. 'You seem annoyed. Was it something I said?'

'No,' said Bertram, going to the door to summon Parry. But I noticed he had left a macaroon on the plate. Bertram is as eager for macaroons as Richenda is for cake. I would like to think that my beloved had sprung new willpower where sweet things were concerned, but from the state of the sugar bowl that seemed unlikely. I wondered who had upset him. I should have to have words with them.

Chapter Eleven
Interviews, Second Sitting

Prentice Davenport sat forward in his chair, a bundle of nervous energy. 'Anything I can do to help,' he said. 'It's all about his missing papers, isn't it? That's what Chapelford said. He suggested that old Killian must have some salacious secret up his sleeve. Not that I would know what that is. Heart attack, was it? Only the others were - well - saying things. Wouldn't be nice for those to get out if it wasn't true.'

Mentally, I kicked myself. I wrote on a piece of paper *We should have got Parry to put them in different rooms after we have interviewed them, so they couldn't confer* and passed it across the table to Bertram.

'Oh, Lord!' said Bertram aloud. He recovered quickly. 'What are your fellows suggesting?'

'That Killian was a bit of a user of drugs - you know, opium and that kind of thing.' He fidgeted in his seat. 'Cole-Sutton was even saying he might have done himself in - excuse me, miss. I know that's not a nice thing to say, especially of a dead man, but I need to be as open and honest as I can be with your employer.'

Out of the corner of my eye I saw Bertram's lips twitch. 'It is very important you tell the truth, Mr Davenport,' I said. 'My sensibilities must come second to justice.'

'Right-o,' said Davenport. 'Thing is, Killian never married, as far as we knew, but when he was in his prime he supposedly was rather fond of the weaker sex. He got very drunk recently and hinted to me of a terrible scandal in his past.'

'When was that?' said Bertram quickly.

'Oh, a couple of nights ago. Let me think. Wednesday, because we had plum duff.' He turned to face me. 'There's always plum duff here on Thursday. It's rather good.'

'Wednesday or Thursday?' I asked.

Davenport slapped himself on the forehead. 'If it's not written down I'm a martyr to my memory,' he said. 'Never could get my head round mathematics at school.'

'What is it you do for a living, Mr Davenport?' I asked.

'I have a little import and export business. Poor Pa popped off quite suddenly. He was in the process of training me up. Then it would have been all fine and dandy, but it wasn't to be. Nasty thing, having a dodgy ticker. Never know when that dreadful chappie with the scythe is going to come calling.'

'Wednesday or Thursday?' said Bertram coldly.

Davenport shook his head. 'Terribly sorry, old thing, but I really couldn't say. Not to put my hand on my heart and all that. Definitely the same day as the plum duff though. So if you ask the kitchen they'll be able to tell you.'

'I'll make a note of that,' I said, hoping we could now move on from puddings.

'Did you ever see Mr Lovelock's memoirs?'

'Yes, that is to say no,' said Davenport.

'Which?' said Bertram, who was beginning to sound more and more like Fitzroy the vaguer Davenport became. The problem was the sterner Bertram was, the more Davenport appeared to want to help him and the more flustered he became.

'I saw him carrying around a briefcase that he said he

kept his scribblings in.'

'But you never saw inside,' I said.

'No.'

'Did Lovelock leave the briefcase lying around?' I asked. 'Could someone less scrupulous than yourself have got a glimpse at the contents?'

'Oh, I don't think any of the members would do something like that,' said Davenport.

'If you could please answer my colleague's question,' said Bertram.

'Well, I suppose they might have done. The lock on it was very simple. You'd only need a cocktail stick to pick it.'

'So, he sometimes left the case unattended?' I said.

'Oh, never,' said Davenport.

'But if he had, you could have picked the lock?' said Bertram.

'Yes. Well, I could have done. Bartle, a boy at school everyone hated, such a swot, used to carry around a briefcase like that. I picked the lock and we filled it full of custard just before prep with Growler Grimes. Ah, school days. They really are the best days of your life, aren't they?'

Beside me I could feel Bertram growing tenser and tenser. 'Why did you join Holby's?' I asked.

'I'm a heritage member,' said Davenport. 'Pa popping off so early, they passed his membership on to me. Jolly good sorts here. I think they knew I'd need a bit of help making contacts for the business. Got two sisters and Ma to support. It's not like I'm the son of a publishing magnate, like Sean Wilkes up at Oxford, having a ball by all accounts.'

'Is that Sebastian Wilkes' son?' I asked.

'That's the chap,' said Davenport. 'Do you know him?'

I shook my head.

'Really? I thought everyone had. Such a prankster! Liable to only get a Third, but what does that matter? He's meeting all the right fellows, and he's got his Pa's newspapers waiting for him when he comes out.' He sighed. 'If Pa hadn't popped off I was meant to go to Cambridge.'

'And read what?' I couldn't stop myself from asking.

'Classics,' said Davenport. 'I presumed it would mean listening to a lot of old music. Could have been a jape.'

After he closed the door behind him Bertram said in a very strained voice, 'Latin and Greek.'

'Probably just as well Pa popped off when he did then,' I said, struggling and failing to contain my laughter.

'That is not funny,' said Bertram chuckling. 'Not funny at all. His poor wife and daughters. Leaving them to the mercy of that clueless imbecile.'

'He seemed a nice clueless imbecile,' I said. 'Do you think he was feigning it, like we think Chapelford was?'

'Sadly no,' said Bertram. 'I think that really was all Pa had to work with.'

'Might be why he popped off early,' I said.

We were both in the throes of merriment when Parry showed in Alistair Cole-Sutton. Now that I saw him standing, I realised he was of no more than average height, but there was a heaviness about him that gave him a stolid presence. 'Have I missed a moment of amusement on this sad day?' he said.

Bertram and I stopped laughing as effectively as if he had poured cold water over us. Cole-Sutton sat down and gave us a big grin. 'Sorry, could not resist,' he said. 'It's been a damn trying day. Wouldn't be surprised if the situation wouldn't have got the better of me under the same circumstances. If you don't laugh, you're not alive, eh? Never know when the Grim Reaper is going to come a calling. Live each day, eh, that's my motto.'

I immediately thought that living each day was preferable to any other alternative, but I kept quiet. I feared for whatever reason I was verging on the edge of hysteria. Perhaps Bertram was right, and it was time for both of us to bow out of this life. Would I miss it? I truly didn't know. It had been better than living at home with Mother on the pig farm and far, far better than being a chamber maid, but how would it compare to the quiet of country life? A waterlogged country life?

'…not much I can tell you about Killian Lovelock,' Cole-Sutton was saying. I took my pencil and attempted to focus. 'He kept himself to himself for most part. You'll know he had soup brought to his writing room every day. That is how I believe they worked out something was wrong. The old gent loved his soup. I certainly saw him carrying his briefcase about. Always tucked under his arm. Tatty old black thing it was. Can't say I ever saw him open it. The rumour was he was writing his memoirs. But you know these older gentlemen, they're coming to the winter of life and they think their family would like something to remember them by - or worse still, posterity does, so they get this idea that they will write a memoir, or a family history, or another version of the battle of Trafalgar. Gives them something to focus on rather than sitting around picking out their coffins and funeral hymns.'

'You think Mr Lovelock was of this type?' said Bertram.

'I'm guessing, I admit,' said Cole-Sutton. 'But the man had apparently spent his whole life pencil-pushing. Now, if that was me, I would be off on my horse the moment the retirement bell rang. Wife says I will die of a broken neck trying to jump a shrub when I'm ninety-two, because that will be all I will be able to manage by them. Great joker, Mrs Cole-Sutton. You would like her, my dear. Everyone does.'

'Pencil pusher?' said Bertram.

'Right, keep to the business. Plenty of time for the social later. Still, that said, wife does a lovely hog roast. You should both come around, bring your mister and missus. We love meeting new people, the wife and I.'

Bertram say nothing. He glowered.

'Right. Right. All I'm saying is, once a pencil pusher, always a pencil pusher. I doubt the man knew what to do with himself when left his office. So that is what he created here. Another little office with plenty of paperwork to do so that there was no chance of him finishing.'

'There has been a comment about him having a reputation as a favourite of the opposite sex when he was younger,' said Bertram. 'Do you know anything about that?'

'Good Lord,' said Cole-Sutton. 'I can't imagine that. But then I have only been a member for two years. Finally let me in when a certain person needed to borrow money and my bank obliged.'

Bertram and I must have looked taken aback, because Cole-Sutton gave a wry smile. 'Not out of the top drawer myself. Wife is as genteel as you please, but she took a few steps down marrying me. Not that we aren't happy and, if I say so myself, the bank is beginning to thrive. All this talk of war - well, let's hope it doesn't come to that, but if it does it will make British banks a lot of money. I say it as one who shouldn't, and woe be to any man who prefers coin over life, but it's the truth. There's a lot of people around who are eyeing this war with greedy eyes.'

'Including you?' said Bertram.

'Not me,' said Cole-Sutton. 'I've got three boys and I don't ever want to see them marching off in a soldier's uniform. Caught a bit of the Boer War myself. Can't say I'd recommend war as a pastime to any man.'

'No, indeed,' I said.

'Thank you, Mr Cole-Sutton, you have been most helpful,' said Bertram.

'Right-o. I will stick around while things get sorted. Call me back any time.' Then he gave a chuckle. 'Almost forgot you locked us in. I won't be going anyway until you say, will I? You devil!' He pointed at Bertram when he said this, but he also gave a huge belly laugh.

After he had left Bertram said, 'What an extraordinary man.'

'I couldn't help think that he looked like Richard,' I said. 'But he is nothing like him.'

'You know, when this is all over, I am almost tempted to take up that invitation for a hog roast.'

'We would have to watch out. His wife is a joker.'

I sighed and leaned back in my seat. 'Only one more to go, and I remain uncertain about everything.'

'You would have thought Fitzroy would have made it here by now. At this rate they'll have to find rooms for us all to sleep in.'

'Do you want to go over the last two interviews?' I said.

Bertram shook his head. 'I have left him to last, but I need to get the Prendergast interview over.'

He had barely said this before Parry opened the door and Prendergast strolled in. He took a seat, crossed his long legs and sat back totally at his ease.

'Well,' he said. 'I trust you have uncovered the murderer by now.'

Chapter Twelve
Bertram and I Deal with a Difficult (ex-)Diplomat

'There has been no mention of murder,' said Bertram firmly.

'I was in the service,' said Prendergast. 'I know a diplomat when I see one. Killian Lovelock might have claimed to be a secretary to some unimportant official, but once you got a few brandies in him that man could discuss and explain complex world events better than any minister I've ever met, and I've met a few.'

'Service?' I queried.

'Diplomatic service,' said Prendergast. 'What did you think I meant?'

'I am merely surprised,' I said. 'You do not strike me as a gentleman overflowing with tact and diplomacy.'

'The question for me is, why did a gentleman of such obvious talent end up in a backwater position. I have no doubt that his last few years were spent in relative obscurity.'

'How so?' asked Bertram.

Prendergast sneered. 'I am not without resources. If he had still moved in the upper diplomatic circles I would have heard of him. In much the same way as I know neither of you work for the Foreign Office. Indeed, the idea of having a woman involved in such things is beyond ridiculous. I recognise you for what you really are.'

To Bertram's credit he did not miss a beat. 'So, you are saying that Lovelock was once a senior diplomat, but that he somehow fell from grace?'

Prendergast nodded slightly. 'That would fit the situation. Of course, he is - was - far older than I, so I cannot tell what happened to him. Presumably it would have been in his memoirs.'

'You think this is why he was killed?' I said.

Prendergast turned his whole body to face only me. 'I have no interest in the affair. I left the diplomatic service after my time in Africa. I did my duty and it brought me nothing but disadvantage.'

'But you said you retained contacts within the service,' said Bertram. 'Either you left, or you did not. You cannot be both in and out.'

Prendergast gave a harsh bark of a laugh. 'But that is exactly what I am. Or, rather, what I do. I run an import and export business, much of which is about supplying our overseas embassies with the delicacies of home. In return they help me import some of the more exotic treasures from the further reaches of our empire.'

'You feel you are owed, after what happened in Africa?' I said.

Prendergast again nodded very slightly. 'That is not for me to say, but certainly there are fellows who believe that I have been unfairly treated.'

'Perhaps you should behave more like a gentleman than a hooligan,' said Bertram sharply. 'You may be answering our questions now, but our earlier acquaintance with you has not shown you in the best light.'

I will not say our subject's eyes glowed red, or that an infernal black smoke arose around him, but there was a change in his demeanour that I would be hard put to quantify, except that I knew his ire rose within him. The knuckles of the hand with which he held his cane went white and his jawline sharpened. I realised he was gritting his teeth. Bertram seemed unaware the man was now as tense as a coiled cobra.

'Why are you answering our questions?' I asked in an attempt to distract him.

'Because I wish to leave this establishment and rescue as much as I can of my business meeting, which should have got under way an hour or so ago.'

I switched tack again, hoping to keep him off guard. 'Did you ever see Lovelock's memoirs, or hear him talk of them?'

'Everyone heard the old fool talk about them. If he wasn't locked in his little room, he would tell all and sundry - even the damn page boys - about the great work he was undertaking.'

'Did he say what he was writing about?' said Bertram.

'His life. That is what a memoir is.'

'We mean,' I said, 'did he ever mention any details?'

'Nothing worth killing him for if that is what you mean. He could talk at length of the wonders of embassy gatherings. The meals. The ladies in their finery. Moving among Europe's elite. I believe he once spun a tale of being sent to Russia. All troikas and caviar. I was not a rapt member of his audience. I come here to relax, and I have no wish to be reminded of my time in the service.'

'But no stories of any great import?' persisted Bertram.

'Not that I heard.'

'Did you ever see the manuscript?' I asked.

'He carried a nasty, tatty little briefcase with him everywhere. Black with a faded gold crest that had almost vanished. What he had inside, apart from his heroin, I could not say.'

'You knew he was a frequent taker of the drug?' said Bertram.

'I suspected. He was of the right age and temperament to wish to relive his youth, and also to have been prescribed the medicine. Perhaps he heard, as I had, that the prescription of heroin is to cease shortly, and he did not wish to live without the euphoria it induced.'

'You know this how?' said Bertram.

Prendergast merely sniffed.

'His ubiquitous contacts,' I said to Bertram. 'The question remains, if Lovelock had been involved in an incident that would shame either the service or certain individuals, had he actually written it down? Considering his use of heroin, did he retain the faculties to be able to do so?'

At this our subject laughed loudly. 'Now that would be priceless,' he said, once he had recovered from his mirth. 'Lovelock killed for something that did not even exist.' He shrugged. 'Still, he was an old man. There are worse ways to die than to go out on a wave of drug-induced euphoria.' He brushed down his right sleeve with his free hand. 'Are we done? I cannot think of anything else I know that would be of interest to you.'

'You did not kill him?' said Bertram.

'I had no reason to,' said Prendergast. 'As I have previously explained, our times in the service did not overlap. Whatever he thought he knew could not harm me.'

'But perhaps one of the people with whom you remain in touch might have asked for your assistance in getting the papers,' I said. 'Perhaps you even found Lovelock, already having overdosed himself, by design or accident, and merely removed the incriminating evidence.'

Prendergast got to his feet. 'I would never do such a thing,' he said. 'I am a gentleman and have the moral code of a gentleman. I am not a dirty little spy.'

Bertram and I failed to answer this insult. Both of us, I believe, were taken aback by the vitriol that dripped from his voice. 'Tell your masters my name and they will tell you that my character is well known. It is impossible for me to behave in such a low manner.'

With this he exited the room. My only condolence was that he took little joy in berating us.

'Couldn't get away from sharing the same air with us fast enough,' said Bertram as the door slammed behind him. 'I'll lay odds that Fitzroy probably does know a thing or two about him.'

'He knows a thing or two about most people,' I said. 'What I want to know is where on earth is he? I am beginning to believe he could not have been in the country when he first telephoned us.'

'That is all too possible,' said Bertram sourly.

'And we are merely to wait at his convenience?' I said.

Bertram reached out and patted my hand. 'Man's a blighter,' he said calmly. 'We know that, but I feel certain he will be happy for us to truss up the right man and lock him in a cupboard somewhere. We can get a couple of policemen to stand guard. There are always a few around this area.'

'It seems we may have to finish this thing alone,' I said sighing. 'I wish we knew whether or not the manuscript existed.'

'Why? It is enough that the killer thought it did.'

'Wilkes said no sensible man would think Lovelock capable of writing his life story,' I said slowly.

'And…' said Bertram, sensing I had more on my mind.

'We could ask among the staff what they thought of Lovelock,' I said, 'but let us suppose for a moment that he

116

may be right.'

'So, it could be that he did accidentally overdose.'

'Oh no,' I said. 'Several people have mentioned he carried a black briefcase with him. That there is no sign of it suggests to me this is murder.'

'You mean the killer did not take the time to check what was in the case?'

'Why take the risk?' I said.

'If Lovelock was under the influence of the drug by his own hand then he might not have noticed,' said Bertram, playing devil's advocate.

'The room was small,' I said. 'Very small. I am happy to say I have never taken heroin, but if it is as has been described…'

'He would be more likely to tackle someone going through his things than lie there in a dreamy state,' finished Bertram for me. 'But that would mean the killer was familiar with the effects of the drug.'

'Most of the members appeared to be so,' I said. 'Perhaps it is more widespread at establishments like the Holby than we have given thought to. Perhaps what Lovelock was doing was, if not encouraged, not discouraged.'

'A safe place to partake,' said Bertram thoughtfully. 'There is something in that. But if there was a chance there was nothing in the briefcase, what does that say about our murderer?'

'Ah, that was what I was coming to,' I said, 'It suggests to me that whoever this man may be, he is very afraid of the memoirs being released. So afraid of whatever Lovelock might write that he was prepared to take the life of a gentleman who the club staff all described as amiable.'

'I don't know about amiable,' said Bertram. 'But in our experience, it has always taken a strong motivation for someone to kill another human being.'

'Except for your brother.'

'Oh yes, him,' said Bertram. 'Well, he's not normal, is he? Most people don't want to kill. Or that is what I believe. You need a damn good reason to get yourself worked up enough to snuff out the life of a fellow being.'

'What about Prendergast and his raging temper?' I said.

'Not the same thing,' said Bertram shaking his head. 'Lovelock showed no signs of violence on his person. Whoever did this not only knew what they were doing but had planned it well.' He shook his head. 'I do not like this. Could it be an assassin from another country?'

'I don't think Fitzroy would have asked you to investigate if he thought there was an assassin involved,' I said.

'He's asked us to keep someone out of harm's way before,' said Bertram. 'Away from such a risk.'

'And we failed,' I said bluntly. 'So he is unlikely to compound his mistake by asking us again. He certainly wouldn't put us at risk by asking us to pursue an assassin.'

'He wouldn't ask you,' said Bertram. 'I agree with that.'

'That is the one thing that has been bothering me,' I said.

'Only one?' said Bertram. '*I* am bothered by the lack of tea, the lack of cake, the lack of moral fibre displayed by all here today, and the very real problem that I may be making such an awful impression on your family that they will forbid our marriage.'

'You are being silly,' I said. 'But you are right, we should order some more tea. This is thirsty work.' I stood up. 'We should also try and find Richenda and check that she has not got herself into difficulty.'

Bertram rose and pulled out my chair. 'So, what is the one thing that bothers you?'

'It is two really,' I said, standing and brushing stale macaroon crumbs from my skirt. 'Firstly, I do not believe I have ever heard Fitzroy so disturbed by a situation. It is hard to put my finger on it exactly, but he sounded...'

'Desperate,' said Bertram.

'Yes. If Lovelock had not been so old I might think Fitzroy was attempting to conceal a mistaken action of his own.'

'If Prendergast is too young to have crossed paths with Lovelock in his prime, we can be certain Fitzroy did not.'

'Too many ifs,' I said. 'But I agree with the principle.'

'And the second thing,' said Bertram escorting me to the door.

'Ah, that. Well, as you said, murder is a desperate act. For someone to be prepared to kill an old man over something that happened a long time ago...'

'It must have been something very bad,' said Bertram.

'Perhaps,' I said. 'No, what I was thinking was that the man who did this, who planned it so carefully and carried out this execution in cold blood, must be very, very afraid. Which makes him profoundly dangerous. He has killed on a rumour. What else might he be prepared to do in order to go free?'

'I had to go and fall in love with an intelligent woman,' said Bertram. 'If only you had been content with embroidery and flower-arranging as occupations.'

I gave him a genuine smile. 'You should be glad. If I had been, not only would you have tired of my company within a year, but you would have had no one to help you in these endeavours.'

'Oh yes,' said Bertram glumly. 'I wouldn't have wanted to miss out on these endeavours.'

Chapter Thirteen
Richenda Resurfaces Resplendently

We had taken no more than a few steps towards our goal of tea and sustenance, when Richenda bowled towards us with all the eagerness of a freight train. 'I have been waiting for you forever,' she said. 'I have much to tell you.'

Bertram groaned and said something under his breath. I could not be sure, but I think it was 'tea', said in tone of a man who sees a desert opening up before him.

'We could discuss this in the coffee lounge,' I suggested.

'I do not believe you will want people to overhear what I have to tell you,' said Richenda, looking rather smug. 'I have struck up an acquaintance with Gilbert Parry. He is the factotum chappie around here. He opened up a little room for me after - well, you should come and see.' Richenda turned and trotted off at a smart pace.

'We could make a dash for the coffee lounge,' whispered Bertram in my ear.

'She might have turned up some important information,' I said. 'Richenda is a lot brighter than most people think.'

'I suppose she would only track us down,' said Bertram. 'Come on then. Where did she go?'

I looked up to see Richenda disappearing down the end of the corridor and around to the right. 'We should get a map of this building,' I said to Bertram. 'We have no real understanding of the places of ingress and express.' We followed Richenda, Bertram's head lowered like a man contemplating his trip to the noose.

'I was hoping it would not come to that,' he said gloomily. 'We will, very shortly, have to ask people who they saw, when and where. We'll have to measure how long it takes to run from A to B and then quantify it by age. Or how stealthy we think the killer was - if there was one. Then we'll have to compare all the clocks and see which one is out by three minutes.'

'I do think, at the very least, we will have to re-interview the suspects,' I said.

'That alone will be jolly unpleasant,' said Bertram. 'They were all pretty clear they didn't enjoy it the first time and us asking them to do it all again is going to be the rancid cherry on the top of their melting ice cream.'

I let this extraordinary statement bypass me. 'I agree it would be useful to know if anyone left the smoking room, and when. I suppose a doctor will be called eventually and he may be able to say when Lovelock died. But what makes you think we should check the clocks?'

'Tedious crime novels I have read,' said Bertram. 'The ones that all depend on noticing some tiny detail, like a misplayed card at bridge, or a cuckoo clock that goes backwards.'

I squeezed his arm. 'But this is real life,' I said. 'We have always found who is at fault by understanding why they did what they did. I do not see why this occasion would be any different.'

'I expect Fitzroy has different rules,' said Bertram.

'Probably, but neither of us are him.'

'Do you mind that?'

'What, not being Fitzroy?' I said. 'I am surprised and rather shocked you would think me capable of being so amoral.'

'I meant my not being Fitzroy.'

'I suppose we might have got an answer more quickly,' I said, 'and not made tedious mistakes like letting our suspects chat together before, and after, the interviews. But he does have vastly more experience in these matters than either of us.'

'Sorry not to be more useful to you,' said Bertram.

I looked up at him, surprised by the bitter tone. 'Are we at odds again?' I enquired. 'I thought we had decided to put aside our differences until after this day's event was concluded.'

Bertram grunted.

'Moreover,' I said. 'I thought we had agreed that whatever differences lay between us, we still were determined to spend the duration of our lives together?'

'That is what you say,' said Bertram. 'But you do not have a spotless reputation for telling the truth, do you, Euphemia?'

I let go of his arm and stopped in my tracks. Bertram carried on. The corridor ended in a discreet carpeted staircase. I gazed up, the stairs wrapped round and round, landing upon landing, spiralling up a good four or five floors. To say we had underestimated the size of this establishment was a masterly understatement. However, Bertram did not falter. He did not offer me his arm again but continued on. 'Look, stairs. Richenda must have got them to take her tea upstairs,' he said as if nothing was wrong.

He began to ascend. I stood there watching him. He did not turn around, so I had little choice, but to follow. I could not think of anything to say. He must be referring to my true status as a lady rather than a servant. It came back to me now that he had made a previous unpleasant comment on my fainting episode, referring to how previously I had never fainted. Did he think I had feigned my faint to get him out of the fight with Prendergast? I thought I had wounded his pride - that The Bishop had been right and he was upset because he could now no longer consider himself as my white knight coming to rescue me from servitude. No, Bertram was hurt that since I had first made his acquaintance, I had lied to him about who I was. As we had grown closer in friendship and eventually fallen in love I had still kept the truth from him. For all the time I had known Bertram, I had lied - until today, when I had no option. He felt distrusted and deceived. This was a much more serious state of affairs that a disagreement over class status. This could shatter the very heart of our relationship.

'Are you coming?' Bertram called over his shoulder.

When I reached the landing one door was open, so I went in. I found myself in what appeared to be a bedroom. Richenda had a tea table set before a nice little hearth that had a small fire burning in it. The room displayed a masculine style with rich red walls, dark wooden seats, a wardrobe, a tallboy and one of those stands that is called an immobile valet or something similar. It is designed to hold all the accoutrements of male attire in a manner designed to facilitate the easy dressing or undressing of a gentleman who may not have his valet with him. I wondered if Bertram would acquire one for himself now Rory had left his employ - and if, the way that things were going, I would ever know.

Richenda had gathered four seats round a table on which were placed the usual tea things, plus yet another tower of tiny sandwiches and cakes. Honestly, I could not but think it would be quicker for the kitchen to cave to pressure and produce a good meal for us all rather than continue to cut up these tiny morsels. Richenda refilled her own cup, and I noticed another used cup on the table. Presumably this had been used by Parry whom she had befriended. I sat down and gratefully took a cup of tea from her.

'So,' said Richenda, 'Mr Parry was kind enough to explain the key system to me.'

'Why, is this a bedroom?' said Bertram, glancing around.

'Country members have the option of staying at the club overnight. Or indeed, as Mr Parry put it to me, members who have enjoyed themselves not too wisely, but too well, and do not want to greet their spouse in their current state…'

'You mean sleep it off here?' said Bertram.

Richenda nodded. 'They offer a valet service for the single gentleman staying. On the upper floors they have suites for couples where both maids and valets are available. However, as one would expect, there is no childcare to be had.' She looked across at me. 'The Bishop must have got special dispensation to bring your brother here today.'

'Perhaps,' I said. 'Or perhaps with it being Ladies' Day, Mr Parry and the club committee felt that letting children in was nothing compared to letting in the fairer sex.'

'It is not a very female-friendly place,' said Richenda. 'If one stays as part of a couple you have to enter through a separate door. They do serve breakfast in the room, but the woman may not descend except to leave! How archaic is that?'

'Gentlemen's Clubs *are* essentially for gentlemen,' said Bertram. 'The clue is in the name.'

Richenda laughed heartily at his response.

'Keys?' I said. 'The key was in Lovelock's pocket. It was assumed he had locked himself in. One of the porters let us in with the master key.'

'Yes, we should have thought more about that,' said Bertram. 'How many master keys are there?'

'Only one,' said Richenda. 'And it is kept on the board behind the desk at reception. This desk is never left unmanned as all the keys are openly on display. If one of the porters needs to answer a call of nature, he must ask the doorman to either find another porter or watch the desk himself. In which case members are forced to open the main door themselves. They do not like this at all, but Mr Parry is most strict. A porter would be instantly dismissed if he left the desk unattended at any point.'

'And if one did, he would not readily admit to it,' I said.

'True,' said Richenda, 'But the training here is regarded as something special, according to Mr Parry. Porters can go from here to work at some significant establishments, and the club's own standards for employment are high. I think it unlikely that a porter had neglected his duty.'

'So, the old man did kill himself,' said Bertram. He sat back in his seat. 'He's put us all to a great deal of trouble, but at least it is all over. We can shut up shop and go home.'

'I do not think so,' said Richenda. 'I was dubious about the keys myself, and as part of my investigation…'

We all paused a moment as I swallowed some tea down the wrong way.

'As I was saying, as part of my investigation I asked Mr Parry to bring me the key Mr Lovelock had used.' Then, like a magician, she produced the key from somewhere within the folds of her skirt. She passed it to Bertram. 'Notice anything?' she said.

Bertram turned it over in his hands. 'Metal. Medium size. Has markings for four tumblers. I suppose it would be possible to pick the lock, if you knew how to do that sort of thing, although if anybody had done so to gain entry to the room, how would they have locked it again afterwards? Any chance the key fits more than one room? If there's a master key, then all the locks have to be similar.'

'I didn't think of that myself, but I was told there are master keys and grand master keys, to help with this. The master key that was used to open Mr Lovelock's room only works on six other rooms on the ground floor.'

'What about skeleton keys?' said Bertram.

'Mr Parry thinks it unlikely that any of the members are liable to be the sort who would have one. To go back a point to your idea that someone might have picked the lock. Mr Lovelock's room was in full sight of a corridor that has other passages and doors leading off it that are in frequent use.'

'I suppose if the matter were not urgent one might attempt to find a time of day when the corridor was in less frequent use, such as luncheon,' I said.

'But the man was always brought soup,' objected Bertram. 'Whoever did it would have a tight window. Oh, Lord, at this rate we will be checking clocks after all.'

'There is a much easier way,' said Richenda. 'I noticed it myself the first time I handled the key.'

Bertram shrugged and passed it to me. Immediately I

felt a substance on the metal. I rubbed two of my fingers together. 'Is it greased?' I said.

'Close,' said Richenda. 'Sniff your fingers.'

'We don't have time for parlour tricks,' said Bertram, but I did as I was told.

'Good heavens,' I said. 'Rose and lavender. It's soap.'

Richenda nodded eagerly. Someone obtained the key - it would only take a moment - and made an impression of it. It would be easy enough to take the impression and slip it back into your pocket without anyone's seeing. It's a shame McLeod isn't here. He would have thought of it, what with that Deacon Brodie fellow.'

'Is he a member?' asked Bertram.

'No,' I said. 'He was a respectable historical figure from Scotland - a carpenter, I think - who made casts of his customers' keys and returned to rob them.'

'Has he been around here?' said Bertram, clearly not following.

'Oh Bertram, he's been dead for centuries!' said Richenda.

'What matters,' I said, 'is you have found a way for someone to copy the key without being suspected. Well done, Richenda. That is an important point and lends credence to the idea Lovelock was murdered.'

'Oh, I have more,' said Richenda with pride. 'There are pictures of all the members over the years displayed on all the floors. I thought if I came down and had a look at who you suspected and,' she swallowed, 'had a look-in on the body, I could see if there were photographs of Lovelock with anyone in particular.'

'Just because they were members of the club at the same time -' began Bertram, but Richenda cut him off.

128

'They do have pictures like that,' she said. 'But there are also group pictures of men from outside the establishment - you know, things like football clubs, rowing teams, even expedition groups.'

'So, you might be able to find one showing Lovelock with people he used to know well. We think that whatever led to his murder is based on something that happened a long time ago,' I said.

'That helps a lot,' said Richenda. 'I could start with the really old daguerreotypes and work forward.'

'Yes,' I said eagerly, 'that would limit your search substantially, but you would still need to view the body.'

'Unless I got Parry to point him out in a photograph,' said Richenda, clapping her hands with delight.

'I do not think Hans would be happy with you associating so much with this fellow,' said Bertram. 'I mean, having tea in a bedroom, alone, with a Club Steward!'

'Oh,' said Richenda laughing. 'That wasn't Parry. He came in and talked to us, but he would never have sat down to take tea, even if I had asked him. He seems as much a stickler for the rules as Stone.'

'Then who…,' I began.

'It is no good,' said Richenda, 'I cannot wait any longer. Here is my pièce de résistance.'

We were both so shocked by what she produced from behind her chair that neither of us even noticed that, for once, Richenda had correctly pronounced her French.

Chapter Fourteen
The Bishop Gives a History Lesson

Bertram and I remained frozen in place as Richenda held the briefcase out in front of her. 'This is it. This is Lovelock's briefcase.'

Then Bertram shot up out of his seat and snatched it from her. He scrabbled at the locks.

'It's empty,' said Richenda, 'I already looked.'

Bertram threw open the top of the case and rummaged around inside it. He found nothing. This annoyed him so much I believe he would have thrown the item down on the table, but for the tea things. Instead he lobbed it towards the fireplace. Fortunately, it fell short. 'Nothing,' he said. 'There is nothing in it.'

I went to retrieve the case.

'I did tell you,' said Richenda. 'Although there may currently be nothing in it, that does not preclude the possibility that there was something in it when it was taken, and removed before the briefcase was discarded.'

Bertram began to pace. The room was small enough that he could not fit in many steps before he had to turn. This annoyed him further. 'It tells us nothing.'

I returned to my seat and examined the briefcase. 'It tells us that someone was in the room with Lovelock before he died. Everyone we have spoken to says he did not let this out of his sight. I think it is even stronger evidence that this is a murder.'

'She is right,' said Richenda. 'Do stop pacing, Bertram. You have your murder.'

'I don't want a murder,' said Bertram crossly, but he stopped pacing.

'I cannot quite make out the crest on the front,' I said, 'but there is a date, eighteen seventy-something. What happened then that a briefcase would be marked to commemorate such a date.'

Richenda held out her hand for the case. 'I didn't spot that,' she said peering at it myopically. 'But I think you are right.' Then she shrugged. 'My knowledge of history is rubbish. Now, if you wanted to know about horses…'

Bertram let out a growl of frustration.

'Go and ask someone who was alive at the time,' said Richenda. 'It is only, oh, thirty-five years ago. There must be hordes of older men who were alive at that time. I mean, even if they were only twenty at the time…' she paused.

'They would be fifty-five now,' I said. 'An age now not considered so very great. Or at least so my mother tells me. I imagine The Bishop is around sixty.'

Bertram swiped the bag off my lap. 'Then let us go and ask your new step father about that time. He strikes me as a man who always reads the *Times* before breakfast.'

'He does, doesn't he?' I said, taking this opening as the sign of an olive branch. However, Bertram got up and left before I had even risen to my feet. I blinked back tears. I said brightly to Richenda, 'You have uncovered the most useful information. Well done.'

'Thank you,' said Richenda. 'Perhaps one day Bertram will agree that I have slightly more brains than my horse. He might even raise my intellectual status to that of a gun dog, as I do seem to be able to ferret things out.'

'Oh, more than that,' I said. 'You put pieces of the puzzle together we had totally missed. Bertram and I have already made several mistakes. We are not used to working with merely the two of us.'

'Especially when you are at odds,' said Richenda gently.

I swallowed hard. 'It transpires that my fiancé has somewhat taken it to heart the fact that I have been lying to him for a number of years.'

'He will get over that,' said Richenda firmly. 'You could never have told us the truth when you turned up looking for a position as a maid at Stapleford Hall. If nothing else, your mother would have - well I am not quite sure what she would have done, but I am certain it would have been drastic and none of us would have enjoyed it.'

'She improves upon acquaintance,' I said.

'Oh, undoubtedly,' said Richenda. 'She is marvellously formidable. I would adore to be just like her. Do you think I should tell her?'

My lips quivered. 'I think you should. She would, at the very least, approve of your ambition!'

Richenda gave a crack of laughter. 'Let us go down together,' she said. 'I can come back up for the pictures later. The last thing you need is your family weighing in on whether you and my little brother have had a disagreement. We shall make it look as if we have been having a girl to girl chat.' Then she looked up at me, surprise dawning on her face. 'We have, have we not? I do not know quite how you managed it, Euphemia, but you have become my dearest friend.'

We embraced, and I sniffed a bit. Richenda sniffed a bit too and scolded me for being sentimental. Then we fixed each other's hair, which had become somewhat ruffled with all the emotion flying around, and made our way downstairs.

We found Bertram and The Bishop seated at a separate table. Richenda nodded at me and went off into the body of the coffee lounge, an expression of determination on her face. I smiled inwardly, wondering if at last my mother had met her match.

I sat down at The Bishop's table and smiled brightly. 'Please excuse my tardiness,' I said. The Bishop had risen at my approach, but Bertram stayed seated peering closely at the briefcase. The Bishop coughed - a most affectingly disapproving cough, and Bertram leapt to his feet to pull out a chair for me.

'I am afraid, my dear,' The Bishop said, 'that at the moment I cannot think of anything especially significant about the 1870s. I was in the process of emerging from seminary and taking my first steps on the ecclesiastical staircase. My thoughts, interests and aspirations were very much taken up with affairs of the Anglican Church. I could probably still recite from the *Church Times* important events in the lives of the British clergy, but that is a small world indeed. As I was telling your betrothed, a large part of my addiction to the *Times* today is to make up for my lack of interest in the world then. I fear the Church has been most remiss in its efforts to bring forth a world of peace.'

'187-something or another,' mused Bertram. 'Or, perhaps, the missing digit is not at the end but at the beginning, say 1187?'

'It is a ragged bag,' I said, 'but I sincerely doubt it is that old.'

'We could ask one of the members?' said Bertram.

'Might you not then be, as they say, showing your hand?' said The Bishop. 'Why do not you ask my wife?'

'Your wife?' said Bertram blankly.

'My mother?' I repeated at more or less the same time.

The Bishop addressed Bertram, 'As you are engaged to my stepdaughter it should not surprise you to learn that my wife is a lady of extraordinary intelligence and insight. We often discuss the *Times* editorial together.'

'And would you agree to that?' I could not help asking.

'Ah, well,' said The Bishop, 'I have always thought the basis of a good marriage is communication and discussion. Partners in life should always challenge each other a little, don't you think? As long as you stand together against the world, then a dash of internal dispute keeps a good relationship thriving. I will fetch her over, shall I?'

'By all means,' said Bertram meekly. I nodded. For as long as I could recall my parents had been at odds. I had assumed my mother resented my father ripping her from her social sphere, but what if she had been restless and bored as a curate's wife? I knew that such a pastoral existence would drive me to despair now I was no longer a child. As The Bishop and my mother came across the room I saw her with new eyes. The pinched look about her eyes and mouth had vanished. She had put on a little weight, but it made her seem more feminine and more relaxed. The Bishop was looking down at her and laughing at something she had said. My mother's expression was a mixture of adoration and irritation. I suddenly thought that perhaps her old phrase, one I always trotted out when I described her, that 'intelligence in a girl is about as much use as a pair of hooves', related more to her fear that I too would become restless and bored. I have loved learning, but had my life not taken an extraordinary turn, I could have ended my days in a miserable marriage where my husband, like many men, saw the feminine love of reading books as a sign of madness and grounds for putting a discontented wife into an asylum. Could that have been the future my mother feared for me? As she sat down I gave her a warm smile. She returned a suspicious look but contented herself with smiling back.

'Now, what are you and young Bertram up to, Euphemia? I am hearing all sorts of stories.'

'My dear, I did suggest not a moment ago that you did not ask this particular question, if you recall,' said The Bishop, seating himself beside my mother.

'There is nothing wrong with my memory, Husband,' said my mother, 'but I think a mother has the right to enquire into the actions of her child.'

'She is assisting me,' said Bertram. 'Euphemia is a remarkably intelligent female, as you will be aware. My instructions come direct from the Foreign Office. I am unable to say more.'

My mother's gaze moved between us. The Bishop patted her hand fondly. She sighed. 'You do not intend to tell me, very well. What would you ask of me?'

'A historical question,' said Bertram. 'You would have been a mere slip of a girl at the time as it was thirty-something years ago.'

'It is not appropriate to make assumptions about a Lady's age,' said my mother. 'However, I believe I would have been around fourteen at the time of the event you are seeking.'

Bertram blinked. 'Oh, of course. Err, I didn't... what... hmm.' He ended this unfortunate speech with a gulp. To my eyes it seemed as if The Bishop gave him a sympathetic look. 'To what event are you referring, my dear?'

'After the Congress of Vienna in 1815,' said my mother. Bertram's eyes bulged. 'For which I was not alive,' said my mother, an acidic note creeping into her voice, 'there were three major peace agreements. Considering the current state of the world, and because The Bishop and I have taken to discussing such matters over breakfast, I decided to look at the previous efforts to make peace with Germany in the hope such a thing could be managed once more in our time.'

'I have no such hope,' said The Bishop sadly. 'To my mind, matters are set upon a disastrous course that there will be no avoiding.'

My mother regarded him respectfully. I mention this merely because the expression on her face at this time was so unfamiliar to me that it took me a moment to realise what it was. It made me wonder if I had ever shown Bertram that I respected his opinion. Perhaps the whole issue about my concealing my status would fade if I showed him how much I valued his opinion. But my mother continued to speak.

'The third and most significant treaty was the Treaty of Berlin. This took place between the thirteenth of June and the thirteenth of July in 1878. It involved Austria, Hungary, France, Germany, Italy, Russia and the Ottoman Empire. It redefined Europe as we know it. The Balkans, in particular, were reformed. Russia gave up much of its recent incursions into the area and ceded back the land. The Ottoman Empire gave up its last European holdings. It was a concerted and effective attempt at creating a geo-political structure to ensure peace in Europe for the foreseeable future. All the countries involved made some sacrifice, but the greatest loser was Bulgaria. They were not then considered a subject of international law, so Russia argued their attendance was superfluous.'

'Even though, as I understand it,' said The Bishop, 'the

whole realm of Bulgaria was reabsorbed and could never then become a sovereign state.' He smiled at his wife. 'I, too, have been doing my homework for our discussions.'

My mother nodded regally. 'I would expect no less.'

'I remember the Bulgaria thing particularly striking me. Some years back, a group of us at the Holby were discussing world events. This must have been 1910 or so. A member was celebrating some kind of anniversary and we had a bit of a bash. Lots of port with postprandial cigars. We were all quite mellow.'

'I see,' said my mother.

The Bishop sensibly avoided her eye. 'I remember quite a heated debate about Bulgaria coming up. Someone had lost their home in Bulgaria, or was it that they had Bulgarian ancestors?' The Bishop rubbed his hand across his eyes. 'Everything of that night is a bit of a fog.'

'Can you remember who was involved in the discussion, sir?' said Bertram eagerly.

'I can't say I even remember much of what I myself said,' said The Bishop dolefully.

'Or even whose anniversary it was?' I asked gently.

The Bishop shrugged. 'It may come back to me, but at this time it is a blank I am afraid.'

'Nevertheless,' said Bertram, 'this conversation has been extremely helpful. Although we - I - must keep an open mind, I think it likely this is a briefcase from that time.'

'That Mr Lovelock held on to it suggests he remembered that time with some fondness,' said my mother. 'Perhaps he was involved in the negotiations somehow? It is a diplomatic bag, is it not?'

'Or he could have been taunting someone, Mother,' I said.

'Gentlemen's Clubs are not my general milieu Euphemia, but I fail to see how one may taunt another with an item of luggage.'

'I fear your daughter means that something may have occurred at the Treaty of Berlin, and that Lovelock was a witness to someone's discredit,' said The Bishop. 'By talk of writing his memoirs, he could be said to be threatening that person, or perhaps even blackmailing him. Very nasty. Whoever it was must be feeling a great deal of relief now he is dead.'

'Euphemia! What a terrible thing to think. Unladylike in the extreme. I despair.' I bowed my head under her stricture. I knew it would be no use pointing out that the deduction had been made by her husband, based on a tangential comment by myself. The Bishop had come close to realising this must be murder. My mother and her new husband were becoming far too involved in what was proving to be a most dangerous game. I looked up at Bertram. He nodded. I felt a frisson as I realised we were thinking the same once more.

'Mrs Hawthorn, my Lord, you have been most helpful,' said Bertram rising.[15] 'But we must detain you no longer…'

'We are finally free to leave?' said my mother.

'I am afraid not,' said Bertram. 'I only meant that this conversation has taken a turn and I wish to relieve you of the burden of following.' He tugged at his collar. It wasn't the neatest phrase, but I had to give credit for originality.'

'And my daughter?'

---

[15]I almost kicked him under the table. It was appropriate for my mother to rise first. He really did not know etiquette beyond what was suitable among bankers and merchants!

Bertram looked at me as if contemplating consigning me to my mother's care. I looked back, willing him to see the fire behind my eyes and the wrath he would unleash if he shut me out of this adventure.

'She has still her duty to dispense,' he said tactfully. Then, with more efficiency than decorum, he left - one might say fled - the table. The Bishop rose and offered his wife his hand. My mother stood and heaved a great sigh.

'I am only glad Joe is too young to be involved in whatever is coming.'

The two of them exchanged polite goodbyes with me, but at the last moment my mother turned back. 'Euphemia,' she said. 'It is not wise to involve oneself with the Foreign Office. The best of men may be led into difficulties. You should speak to Bertram if you are serious about this engagement.'

'I have done so today,' I said, surprise making me blurt out the truth. 'We have decided to ensure we are not called upon again.'

'Very wise,' said my mother. 'After all, now the police are here, you must be able to hand over your task.'

I looked wildly around the room. 'The police?' I echoed. 'I have no knowledge…'

'Oh, not in this room, but Richenda was telling us about the very nice policeman she had tea with. She was able to brief him quite thoroughly about the situation. A remarkable woman. I cannot say I like the sound of that husband of hers. I believe he is not English?'

'German,' I said. 'On his father's side, but he conducts himself with the all the decorum of a gentleman.'

'I should hope so, as I understand you are a guest in his house. Younger than her, too? I suppose she thought life was passing her by?' said my mother. 'The coming war will prove difficult for them both. Perhaps you should speak to the Foreign Office about protecting her. After all, she is a British citizen.'

'So is Hans,' I said crossly. 'He is every bit as English as I am.'

'Nonsense,' said my mother. 'You have an excellent pedigree.'

'Like a horse,' I snapped back.

'Come, Husband, let us find some tea and refined company. I must apologise for my daughter's manners. She has been regrettably away from my influence for some years and it does not appear she has consorted with the best of people.'

The Bishop blinked at this. He looked between us. 'Ladies, this is a stressful occasion. I trust we will have a pleasant meal and discussion at another time when all bad feelings will have evaporated in the milk of good Christian kindness.'

My mother and I snorted in unison and turned from each other. I was greatly tempted to turn back and see what The Bishop made of us both. However, I suspected he would have pretended not to notice anything was wrong and would fail to indulge my mother in any gossip over my conduct. He seemed a most diplomatic gentleman, but unlike my father, I had already seen he was more than prepared to stand up to my mother when he thought it necessary. Presumably, when encouraging her to be kinder, he could quote God as being on his side. If only my father had tried that - but he had simply adored her, once.

I did eventually turn and watch my mother walk away, her back straighter than any soldier's. It was a slight stretch for her to reach The Bishop's arm with her so tiny and him so tall. She did not turn back. I felt a genuine warmth for the two of them as I watched him slow his pace to hers and lean down to hear her, while she speeded up her walk to a trot and stood on tiptoe to speak to him.[16]

I shook my head. Police? There was no one present that I could identify as such. Perhaps my mother had been mistaken. I could ask Richenda, but then I risked being drawn into another family conversation. I decided to go and ask Evans at the front desk. Presumably he, of all people, would know if a policeman had been let in by Watts the doorman.

I found Evans at his post. I had not even opened my mouth when he said, 'He's through the back,' and indicated what I had taken to be a porter's cubby of some kind. Evans raised a section of the desk and I passed through. He ushered me towards the cubby. I entered, about to berate any policeman for not informing us of his presence.

A man sat at a small desk with piles of tomes scattered around him. He carried on scoring out a line in an open volume with an ink pen before looking up. 'Nice to see you, Euphemia,' said Fitzroy. 'How has your day been? Mine has been an absolute rotter.'

---

[16]It also occurred to me they would make an excellent subject for the *Times'* cartoonist.

Chapter Fifteen
Fitzroy is Remarkably Informative

'Fitzroy!' I said, torn between relief and anger. 'What on earth are you doing?'

The spy raised an eyebrow. 'What does it look like? I am amending the record of members.'

'Have you no shame!' I said.

Fitzroy cocked his head on one side, appearing to consider my question seriously. 'I do not believe so. It would be most cumbersome in my occupation.'

'I can imagine.'

'Redacting.'

'Excuse me?'

'What I am doing it is called redacting. I am removing names on behalf of the Crown.'

'Do you mean a member of the Royal family is on the membership rolls?'

'I couldn't possibly tell you that. Now, draw up a chair and tell me how you are faring. I confess I am also being distracted by the notion of you marrying a sheep. If we cleared that up I believe I could focus more easily on the matter at hand.'

I pulled over a chair. I knew better than to wait for Fitzroy to do it for me. 'You are teasing me,' I said.

'Perhaps a little, but it is a most arresting image.'

'My mother...'

'Is she still here?' interrupted Fitzroy.

'In the coffee lounge.'

'Damn, we should probably let those people go. Is it

your mother who wants you to marry a sheep?'

'No, but if I do not marry Bertram then I will be required to live in The Bishop's Palace and marry an older, sensible, and sobering suitor.'

'Ah, hence the sheep. I see. I think it would be a far better idea to marry Bertram.'

'Perhaps you might care to explain that to him,' I said.

'If necessary I will so instruct him,' said Fitzroy in a voice that boded ill for the absent Bertram. 'But for now, we have a murder to solve. Richenda was most informative. By the way, she thinks I am a plain clothes detective. Please do not disabuse her of this notion. I understand that Lovelock's memoirs are at the heart of the case, but as yet we do not know if they even exist. I take it you have considered blackmail?'

I nodded. 'A moment ago. But if that was so, there must have an incident that made the murderer take action.'

'A tipping point,' said Fitzroy, angling the pages I was attempting to surreptitiously read away from me.

'He had been parading around with the briefcase for some time according to the members.'

'If he was about to complete the manuscript, or worse, had engaged with a publisher, then it would be time for the murderer to act.'

'Why should Lovelock engage with a publisher?' I said.

'Exactly,' said Fitzroy. 'If the purpose of his enterprise was to increase his personal funds only an offer of significant payment would entice him to publish. Regular payments from blackmail are often thought preferable to a single lump payment, unless it is very large.'

'And if he was blackmailing someone then he would have to realise that if the blackmailee - is that a word? - might be liable to take serious action, and would he not then take great precautions not to let that individual know that his secrets were about to be cast upon the world?'

Fitzroy gave me a charming smile, reminding me he could be most engaging when he wished. I immediately felt worried. What did he now require me to do?

'What?' I said warily.

The spy shook his head. 'I was merely thinking that if you had been born a man, what an asset you would have been to my department.'

'I thought I was an asset,' I said, feeling annoyed despite my avowed decision to back away from this work.

'You are,' said Fitzroy, 'But I am limited in the ways I can utilise you. British society is still in fear of intelligent women. Anyway, back to Lovelock: we have to factor in his addiction.'

'That heroin makes a user feel heroic, I know. As a long-term user, he might have felt himself to be superhumanly empowered and thus safe from his blackmail target.'

'It is a tangle,' said Fitzroy. 'I have people searching discreetly for the manuscript, but I do not hold out much hope of finding it. The briefcase was discarded in an empty room upstairs. Possibly the person who left it there wanted us to believe it was empty all along but, bearing in mind I suspect our culprit was once an agent himself, they may be sending a message that it is gone and we should leave well alone. I suppose the time has come to tell you that the department has no wish for the contents of the manuscript to be released into the public arena either.'

'You would let a murderer go free?'

'I would prefer not to,' said Fitzroy. 'My response to

blackmail is never to pay.'

'Let them publish and be damned?'

'A more permanent solution is generally preferable.'

I raised my eyebrows. 'You don't need to speak in euphemisms with me, Eric. I have played my part, even peripherally, in your world for long enough for my innocence to no longer be an issue.'

Fitzroy closed the tome in front of him with a slam. 'That is not something I ever intended.'

I shrugged. 'What do you know of the Treaty of Berlin?'

Fitzroy paled. He recovered quickly, but I saw the shock on his face. 'We are right, aren't we?' I said. 'It is all about something that happened between June 13th and July 13th 1878 in Berlin, isn't it?'

'Not exactly,' said Fitzroy. 'I suspect it concerns an event that occurred around June 10th 1878.'

'Then you must know who was involved,' I said angrily. 'Why have you kept us in the dark?'

Fitzroy stood abruptly and began to pace around the small confines of the room. I had seen him like this before. It usually meant that something was troubling him deeply - and generally it was something he was trying like the devil not to let me know. 'There was an incident, a diplomatic one.'

'Concerning Bulgaria?' I hazarded.

Fitzroy paused momentarily, but his back was to me, so I could not see his expression. Then he continued to pace. 'Possibly,' he said. 'However, while I know the names of many of those involved, I only know the codename of the man I believe to be responsible.' He turned and looked at me, an expression of sadness, or even apology, on his face, 'As you will have realised, I am far too young to have been at the event in question. When I inherited the situation from Hyperion, my superior at the time, years ago, I looked over a file on the incident and made the decision that no further action was required. The case appeared to be stagnant and I had far more pressing concerns on my time. I may have been too hasty. I did not make a connection that I should have done until it was too late.'

'I don't understand,' I said. Fitzroy sat down again and fiddled with the edge of one of the ledgers. 'What was the codename for the agent you suspect?' I asked.

'Helios. Greek word for...'

'The Sun. I know, my father taught me Greek.'

Fitzroy gave me an odd look I could not read.

'Did he have a particularly fiery temper?' I asked lightly.

'What he had was Pyrois, Aeos, Aethon and Phlegon, codenames for the civilian assets under his remit. From what I read in the file, Phlegon was a traitor, working for a foreign agency, the Russians. For reasons unknown to us he must have displeased them, and they murdered him. Fearing that the identity of the other assets might have been compromised by him, the whole team was pulled out and a new one sent in. Helios disappeared, with the department's blessing, and the assets returned to be reintegrated into normal civilian life with our help.'

I frowned. 'And what does Hyperion think?'

'He died a long time ago. An ailment of old age, but he never gave any thought to writing a memoir, private or otherwise. It would have made my life a hell of a lot easier had he done so. Spies aren't the most trusting of people - even with other spies. Hyperion took many of his secrets to the grave, including the identity of Helios.'

'And you have been picking up the pieces ever since?' I asked.

'On occasion,' said Fitzroy. 'What was a damaging secret once can fade into a minor embarrassment, or even into a mostly ignored footnote to history.'

'But not all of them?'

'No. Sadly, actions taken in this business can have repercussions down the decades.'

'For whom?' I asked.

Fitzroy sighed. 'In my experience, those who did not deserve them.'

'So, in a sense you are clearing house?' I said.

'When I am not trying to prevent a war with Germany that will see a loss of life the like of which most people today could not even imagine.'

'It must be difficult for you,' I said.

'What?'

'Everything,' I said with a smile. Fitzroy laughed. 'Well, you understand more than most. That's something I suppose.'

'What happened to Pyrois, Aeos, and Aethon?' I asked.

Fitzroy's face hardened. 'All dead,' he said. 'That is what I missed. I tried to warn the last of them, but...'

'So, was Lovelock one of these three?'

'No, and that is part of why I almost missed him entirely. He was stationed at the British Embassy at the time, as a junior secretary. He helped cover up the - incident - in Berlin. He was sidelined afterwards into general posts. I think it was hoped he'd never put all the pieces together.'

'But he did.'

Fitzroy nodded. 'I fear so. He must also have realised his career has been stymied because of what he had seen and heard.'

'So, the memoirs were revenge?' I asked.

'Possibly,' said Fitzroy. 'He could make himself a man of the moment by revealing what Phlegon did - if he did anything that is.'

'You mean you suspect that Helios did whatever it was that created this incident and laid the blame on Phlegon?'

Fitzroy smiled once more. 'Yes. At the time it was believed that Phlegon was exposed as a double agent for Russia. He was to be rewarded with lands in New Bulgaria.'

'How did he get Phlegon to shoulder the blame – oh,' I said. 'He killed him, didn't he?'

'Yes,' said Fitzroy. 'Helios claimed he caught on to Phlegon betraying his country. Only now I believe it was the other way around. At the time Helios' standing was such in the department that no one ever considered he could be the traitor.'

'You said you tried to warn the last of them,' I said thinking back. 'Do you mean Helios killed the other three civilian assets? How was that not noticed?'

'You mean how did I miss that? Because he took his time. He was patient and he was careful. He must have kept watch on the assets and, over time, discreetly dealt with what he believed were the only people who could have worked out the truth. We had similar training, so I know much of what he is capable,' said Fitzroy.

'Set a devil to catch a devil?' I suggested. I tried to keep my tone light, but this history was disturbing me deeply. I had never witnessed Fitzroy blame himself for, well, anything. The resulting mood it engendered in him was darker and more vengeful than I had seen before. I will not say I was afraid of him at that moment, but I took comfort from knowing others were within earshot.

The door opened. I turned, expecting to have to repulse Evans, only to see Bertram on the threshold. His face was full of the excitement of discovery. 'Euphemia,' he cried looking at me. 'I have been looking for you everywhere. I have discovered a strange substance was added to the fire in the smoking room. It appears to have made the smoke thicker than usual. It is undoubtedly a murder.' Then he registered the man sitting beside me. 'You,' he said, 'how long have you been here?'

'Long enough,' said Fitzroy, 'to know this day will not end well.'

Chapter Sixteen
I Research More Deeply into the Puzzle and Bertram is Very Cross

Bertram came into the room and perched on the edge of the table where the ledgers were. I could not help feeling it was like watching two dogs vying for superiority. Although this gave Bertram the greater height, he clearly demonstrated it was not a comfortable position. Fitzroy, in contrast, merely leaned back in his chair, very much at his ease.

'It's all very well for the two of you to get excited over the fact this is almost certainly a murder, but if you are correct then you also have to catch the criminal,' said Fitzroy.

'But you are here now,' said Bertram. 'Euphemia has doubtless told you everything, as she always does. I presume you always knew she was the granddaughter of an Earl. You probably even know the Earl.'

'I do,' said Fitzroy pouring petrol on the fire. 'and I did. It is my job to stay abreast of events.'

'As it is my role to stay in ignorance,' said Bertram, more or less falling off his perch. He staggered slightly but kept his dignity intact.

'It is good to hear you noticed the residue in the fire. I too noticed that after I had viewed the body. Poor old Lovelock has been indulging in his magic medicine for many years. I had not imagined he would be so frail. It really would not have been difficult for the killer to give him the extra dose. I take it you found the second injection site? Like most addicts he injected in his foot, near the base of his toes.' Fitzroy indicated the area on his immaculate brogue. 'Whereas the murderer left a pin prick in his arm. Clearly not a user himself. In fact, someone so ignorant of heroin use might almost be said to abhor it.'

'As you do,' I guessed.

Fitzroy nodded.

'So, another piece of evidence pointing at Helios,' I said.

'Indeed. Now, I have security matters to attend to. If you could root out the murderer that would be excellent,' said Fitzroy, rising.

'We had a thought earlier that it might be the son of someone, rather than the man himself.'

Fitzroy hesitated. 'I am unaware that Helios ever had family.'

'Because you have chosen to be single does not mean he did,' I said.

Fitzroy frowned. 'It would be a singularly selfish man to beget a family doing the work we do.'

I laughed. 'You already said the man is a traitor, so why is it so difficult to comprehend that he is selfish too? Is not the whole basis of being a traitor that one rates someone or something else above one's country?'

'Yes and no,' said Fitzroy. 'People may betray their country for a variety of reasons. Love is one of the worst.' He gave himself a slight shake. 'I do hope you are wrong, Euphemia. It would complicate matters to a level that... What is the matter with you?' he addressed Bertram.

'I am furious,' said Bertram. I turned to see a deep scowl on his face. He held himself rigid with suppressed passion. 'I have had enough of being your lackey.'

Fitzroy breathed a sigh of deep exasperation. 'Not

now,' he said. He moved to leave the room, but Bertram remained in his way. 'Explain things to him, Euphemia,' said the spy, as he brushed roughly past Bertram. His impact on Bertram's shoulder was audible. My fiancée gave a little grunt of pain and then flushed in embarrassment, but Fitzroy had left the room.

'You had better sit down,' I said, pretending not to notice the clash. 'He relayed a lot of information.'

Bertram sat down, still scowling. 'Why am I not surprised?' he said.

It took some minutes to catch Bertram up with everything I had been told. I also found myself going back over details and correcting myself. It was not as if Fitzroy had allowed me to make notes. To do Bertram justice, despite his temper, he listened intently and asked a few pertinent questions.

When I finished he looked a little startled. 'So, we are on the trail of a multiple killer?' he said.

'I hadn't thought of it like that,' I said. 'But I suppose we are. If Fitzroy is right, the motive all the way along has been to prevent the leaking of certain events surrounding the Treaty of Berlin from the British envoy.'

'Except he did not quite finish telling you that, did he? You said he mentioned something about it not being between the dates we were given for the treaty? And that also, in more recent years, he attempted to warn someone who was an innocent civilian asset, but who died anyway. Murdered? He didn't give you a name, did he?'

'He isn't being his normal thorough self,' I said. 'Altogether, he is rather out of sorts.'

'Why? Did his dog die?' said Bertram with no sympathy.

'I have no idea.'

'Anyway, the less said about that dreadful man the better. As soon as this is all over you can put him out of our lives.'

I felt a twinge of regret but managed to suppress it. Bertram was talking about our lives together again and that would have to content me. That I felt most discontented about leaving Fitzroy's world, with its puzzles and intrigues, would be something I would have to keep to myself if I ever wished to tie the knot with Bertram. Involuntarily I sighed.

'What?' said Bertram sharply.

I thought quickly. 'You are right, we still have a tangle to unravel, and while we have new information I do not think it moves us on very far. If at all. This has to be about loss and gain. Undertaking this murder, if Fitzroy is correct, is part of a long game Helios has been playing. He is tidying away the evidence bit by bit. Why? Fitzroy's department no longer even know his real name. Whoever Helios is, he has a new life and new identity. And yet, he has chosen to kill Lovelock.'

'Presumably because Lovelock knows who he is and what he has done,' said Bertram.

'But then why not go to the relevant authorities?' I said. 'I mean, the average person might not know who to approach, but someone who has moved in government and civil service circles presumably would.'

'Unless he thought there was a spy there,' said Bertram.

This made me laugh. Gradually a smile dawned on Bertram's face. 'I see what you mean,' he said chuckling. 'If anything, we have too many of the wretches.'

'If I have this right, Helios has been systematically eliminating all those who may have been witness to his treachery or, at the very least, those who know enough to have the capacity to put the pieces together and uncover the truth. We can assume something went wrong with his own plans…'

'And he made Phlegon his stooge,' said Bertram. 'But how does Fitzroy know this?'

'Only because all the other assets have since died, and while he didn't say so, I assume he meant in unnatural circumstances.'

'Not so unnatural that the police would notice, but…'

'Fitzroy, who was beginning to join the dots on this old file, did. Lovelock was his last living link, but I don't think he was one of Helios' team.' I shook my head. 'My head is aching with all this.'

'Let us simply assume Helios, or his descendants, don't want his treachery known. Why?'

'Executed as a traitor, removal of assets, loss of family reputation,' I said.

'That's what I think,' said Bertram. 'I think Helios is thinking of his next generation. He must be an old man by now. If he has a son to carry on his name…'

'Fitzroy said something about the worst crimes being committed for love.'

'Did he?' said Bertram not sounding very interested. 'Let us have a think about who among our suspects are family men…'

'Or their sons,' I said. 'Prentice Davenport said himself he had inherited unexpectedly. What if his father confessed on his death bed and he is trying to clear up the mess?'

'Not impossible,' said Bertram. 'But it's rather like a melodrama.'

'Sebastian Wilkes is old enough to have fathered a number of children,' I said.

'The rest of them are the right age too,' said Bertram. 'We could look in the members' registers and see if they list whether or not members are married?' He gestured at the books Fitzroy had been amending.

'I caught Fitzroy writing in those,' I said.

'That's jolly interesting,' said Bertram sitting up. 'What did he say he was doing.'

'Removing information.'

Bertram gave a bark of reluctant laughter. 'Sometimes I can't help liking the fellow.'

'Ma'am,' said Evans from the doorway, 'you can't go in there.'

'Stop me if you dare,' said Richenda's voice. She waltzed in and dumped herself down on Fitzroy's vacated chair. It creaked in protest.

'I am so tired,' she said. 'I've been popping in and out of that lift like Amy's jack-in-the-box toy. Wretched thing always made me feel dizzy watching it.'

'Why?' asked Bertram.

'The way it bounces up and down - and no matter how many times I see it jump up when the lever is depressed, it always startles me.'

'I meant why were you getting in and out of the lift?' said Bertram.

'I've been looking at the photographs, but to be honest I don't know what I am looking for. I got one of the porters to point out Lovelock to me in a picture and then I began searching for other ones with him in. But I haven't noticed anything unusual. I think I should meet your suspects.'

'Probably,' I conceded at the same moment as Bertram uttered an emphatic, 'No.'

'I should tell you that we know our murderer only by a

codename he once used - Helios,' I said. Bertram shot me a filthy look.

'Oh, how delicious,' said Richenda. 'Does that mean the victim didn't know his real name either? Because if he didn't, how could he write about him?'

'If he had known Helios' real name he would have known to avoid him…' I said. 'Richenda, you're brilliant. Lovelock didn't know Helios was here! That explains so much.'

'It does?' said Bertram.

'The last time he saw him was decades ago and Fitzroy said he took on a new identity afterwards,' I said.

Bertram clapped his hand to his forehead. 'What if Lovelock was writing the truth about what actually happened? What if this was all about clearing Phlegon's name?'

I nodded. 'Yes, Fitzroy realised afterwards Helios was the traitor, but I don't get the impression this has ever been officially acknowledged.'

'You've lost me,' said Richenda. 'And I thought I was doing so well.'

'Lovelock hasn't seen Helios since 1878. Helios took on a new identity,' I explained as succinctly as I could.

'Well, then I've been wasting my time looking at old photos,' said Richenda. 'He would have to have joined the Holby recently or Lovelock would know him.'

'Dash it,' said Bertram. 'She's right. Euphemia, go through the ledgers and find out who of our suspects joined recently. Richenda, you should go and refresh yourself with cake. You've been brilliant. I am going to go and confront Fitzroy with our reasoning.'

They both departed with some eagerness. Richenda's was self-evident and I suspected Bertram thought he had got one up on Fitzroy. I doubted that and would have detained him if I had thought of a way to do so without damaging his pride. I hoped he confronted Fitzroy alone. In my experience, although the spy might not yet know the answers to a puzzle, he considered everything. I had no intention of seeking them out. Fitzroy would not be kind when putting Bertram in his place and the last thing Bertram would need would be me witnessing that.

I pulled over the ledger that the spy had been writing in. He had closed it - and blotted the ink while I was in the room - so I did not think I would be able to easily find what he had redacted. I turned the ledger on its side. Embossed in gold print along the black leather spine it read *New Members 1870-1880*. Whoever Fitzroy had been removing from the membership list, it had not been a recently joined member. This suggested the spy was up to his nefarious games again, but in this case, I had neither need nor want to know what it was.

I closed this ledger and moved it to one side. The books were oblong in shape and despite being bound they were all handwritten. Columns read name of applicant, address of applicant, occupation of applicant, date of application, sponsor, accepted/rejected. The script in any book, I quickly discovered, was liable to be the same throughout. Could this be the job of the Honorary Secretary, to write them all? I confess the idea of uncovering Lawrence Prendergast as the culprit disturbed me far less that it transpiring to be one of the more seemingly likeable gentlemen.

The pages were a dull light blue and the lines of the columns and rows in navy. The script was all in black, save for the accepted/rejected column, where rejected was written in red. I worked my way back from the present day to 1890, by which time my right eye had begun to twitch uncontrollably. The handwriting was cramped and small, and more than once I had to lean closely over the ledger to make out a name. I found only one incident of a rejection, a Martin Pippenny, who listed his occupation as owner of a department store. Generally, the members were civil servants, doctors, lawyers, clergymen, banking merchants, and import and export men, with only Gordon Chapelford listed as a Chartered Accountant. I noted he had been sponsored by Prentice Davenport's father, Alfred, in 1901. Prentice himself was listed as a heritage member some years later. This must rule out Prentice. I had not found the listing for Alfred as a new member, so he must have joined as a young man. Thus, Lovelock would have had no issue with identifying him. I felt we could rule Prentice out on his own account due to his youth and his father being a long-standing member.

Lawrence Prendergast had been sponsored in 1905 by a name I did not recognise. I did not think this could clear him. Although, admittedly, he might be a bit young to be Helios. I wondered how I could ascertain his actual age. Guessing the age of gentlemen over thirty was not something I felt confident in doing. Some men appeared to age much faster than others. Having spent time in Africa, the sun had taken its toll on his skin, enough to make him appear older than he was. However, Bertram had thought him too young, and a fellow member of his sex no doubt had a better eye for maturity than I.

Gordon Chapelford had been put up for membership by Alfred Davenport in 1891. He was an oddity among the upper middle-class professions of the other members. I recalled that someone had suggested he might have helped a member out of financial difficulties by loading his books but, if so, would that man leave a trail of suspicion by attaching his name to a proposal? Personally, I would have been more careful. However, I could hardly ask Alfred, and I had already ruled out the Davenports. On the whole, Chapelford felt wrong to me. The way he had conducted himself in the interview aside, I thought he was hiding something, but that could be a criminal prosperity that had nothing to do with Lovelock's murder.

Alistair Cole-Sutton had been accepted in the Holby club in 1910, a mere three years previously. His sponsor had been Prendergast, who had not only admitted to being in the diplomatic service himself but retained contacts therein. Could he have come across Cole-Sutton before, during his time in the service? I needed to know from Fitzroy how common it was for agents and diplomats to exit either service with a new identity. Could Prendergast have been helping Helios re-establish himself as Cole-Sutton? I felt I was clutching at straws. I had the grace to admit to myself that I wanted Prendergast to turn out to be on the wrong side because he was so unpleasant. Cole-Sutton, by contrast, had been amiable enough during his interview, not only to invite us to a hog roast, but to have both Bertram and me considering going. He had come across as open, honest, and being as helpful as he could. He had offered sensible theories and spoken of his wife and family with great affection. Of course, that gave him a family reputation to safeguard.

Sebastian Wilkes I found had, surprisingly, only joined the Holby in 1911. His sponsor was another name unknown to me. I flicked back through the volume I had concentrated on but found no mention of the sponsor. Obviously, another long standing-member. But then I thought Wilkes to be the oldest of all of them, so it was of no surprise he might have older friends. I thought back to his interview, he had been a complete gentleman - something Fitzroy never was. If they were once in the same line of business, they would have had very different approaches. This didn't preclude Wilkes from being Helios, but I had difficulty imaging such a perfectly mannered specimen of civility and etiquette coming from the same stock as Fitzroy. He had had a commanding presence and had been much more in control of the interview than Bertram - but if he was the captain of industry he claimed to be, would that not fit him playing his new character?

I sat back and massaged my temples. I felt there was a glimmer of light ahead, but it was still very faint. There were ideas at the edge of my mind that would not come into proper focus. I had too much information. I turned to my notes from the interview and started to underline and add to the parts I felt were of significance. Perhaps if I could abstract the essence into a small table or diagram I would begin to see things more clearly. Or at least be able to latch on to what was nagging me at the back of my mind.

Lawrence Prendergast

Joined 1905. Elected Hon Sec 1906. Despite current (irate/violent) demeanour must be agreeable to members. Would have had easy access to membership ledgers and all information within.

Age? Skin prematurely aged in Africa, or older than he looks. Said he was convinced Killian Lovelock was more than a civil servant. Why draw attention to himself like that? Spoke of diplomatic contacts and time in the service.

Prentice Davenport

Heritage member, very young and, from interview, not the quickest intellectually. His father, Alfred, joined before 1870, and would have known Lovelock for some time. Father Alfred sponsored Gordon Chapelford.

Gordon Chapelford

Cannot dismiss feeling there is something sorely amiss with this character, but it may have nothing to do with Lovelock's murder. Joined in 1901. Very much the odd man out, both by class and by profession. Appeared an almost comic-like caricature of a lower middle-class gent. Only suspect to claim having seen Lovelock's actual papers.

Sebastian Wilkes

Only a member since 1911. Sponsored by another older man. Confident and controlling. However, extremely well-mannered, in complete contrast to Fitzroy. Seems unlikely they both have/had the same occupation (it is not one for a gentleman). Manners from a bygone age. Prentice mentioned he had a son at Oxford.

Alistair Cole-Sutton

Joined in 1910, sponsored by Prendergast. Has three sons. Very amiable character, working in banking. Seemed certain the papers must exist but had never actually seen them. Suggested it was in Lovelock's character to keep doing paperwork. Given Prendergast's claim he still has diplomatic contacts could be helping Cole-Sutton evolve new identity, but timing is strange. Grounds for suspicion, except Cole-Sutton's friendly demeanour is most convincing.

Cannot tell from notes whether it was Prendergast or Wilkes who first suggested the actual memoirs might not exist. Cannot remember either. Damn!

I put my pencil down and regarded my little table. Leaving aside my personal preferences, I could only rule out the Davenports. I would have to count that as progress. If I stared at these reports any longer I would give myself a bad headache. I closed the notebook and put it in my skirt pocket.[17] Despite the urn-full of tea I was sure I had swallowed that day, I felt badly in need of more.

I was about to get to my feet when Richenda once more burst in upon me. 'Oh, good heavens!' she cried. 'I didn't know what to do. Your mother has been taken quite unwell.'

My heart pounded in my chest. 'What has happened? Is it her heart?'

'Oh no, nothing like that,' said Richenda. 'I think she is merely distressed over seeing your father again.'

'The Bishop?' I said.

'No, your real father. Josiah Martins.'

'My father?' For the second time that day I fainted completely away.

---

[17]The advantage of having a seamstress to fit the occasional pocket into a full skirt cannot be denied. It was only when Richenda insisted that the pockets be attached to every garment that the concept became garish.

Chapter Seventeen
Fitzroy and I Have a Private Conversation of Some Import

'Really, Euphemia,' said Fitzroy's voice. 'I fear this is a most unbecoming new habit.'

I opened my eyes to find myself back in the ladies' powder room, back on the same chaise where I had been laid out before. Fitzroy had a damp flannel in his hand, which he applied to my forehead. The acute pain in my head receded to a moderate one.

'Where is Bertram?' I asked.

'Elsewhere,' said Fitzroy. 'Would you like a glass of water, or a glass of brandy?'

I inched myself up against the side of the chair. My head felt woozy. 'Take it slowly,' warned Fitzroy. 'I can't find any sign of head injury, but Richenda seems to think you hit your head on the table. She was a little hysterical, so it was difficult to understand what she was saying. Is she often like that? I do pity Hans.'

He picked up a lit lamp from a nearby table and held it near my face. He peered uncomfortably closely into my face. He moved the lamp from side to side. 'Well, your eyes are reacting to the light like normal.'

'What does that mean?' I asked.

Fitzroy shrugged. 'Not sure. I only know that if they don't I'd need to get you to a doctor quickly.' He smiled at me. 'I very much enjoyed reading your assessment of the case. I think, with a little training, you could be a lot of help during interviews and analysis. You show a natural, if unrefined, talent for it.'

'You read my notebook?' I said. 'That was in my pocket!'

'Yes, I felt it when I carried you here.'

'You searched me!' I said appalled.

'No, I told you. I felt it when you were in my arms. I knew exactly where it was. There was no need for me to search you. For once I have behaved as a gentleman,' he said with a rueful smile. I remembered some of the things I had written and felt myself blush. Fitzroy turned away, so he could pretend not to see my embarrassment.

'Before you attempt to rise, let me assure you that Richenda is a fool and your mother is not a bigamist. Your father, I am sorry to say, remains very much dead.'

It was only when he said this that I remembered why I had fainted. I felt my throat close and a prickle of tears at the back of my eyes. 'Even when we hear something we know to be ridiculous,' said Fitzroy kindly, 'we cannot help but hope.' He sighed. 'I did try to deal with this, but I did not count on Richenda and your mother becoming such firm friends. She took your mother for a turn around the club.'

'She saw a photograph,' I managed to say. I still felt stupidly tearful. Again, Fitzroy turned his gaze away from me and onto the opposite wall.

'Exactly. Before your father ever met your mother, he was a member of the Holby. It was his name you caught me redacting. I did not wish to open up old wounds.'

'But he was only a country curate,' I said. 'I have read the professions of the other members…'

'You forget, Euphemia, they also had heritage members. Your father gained his membership because your paternal grandfather was a member.'

'I have never met him.'

Fitzroy's shoulders slumped. He suddenly looked very tired. As he placed the lamp back down, his face looked haggard and lined. 'I am sorry then to tell you that you never will. Your father was their younger son. His parents are both long gone.'

'He had siblings? I have uncles and aunts I have not met?'

Fitzroy drew up a chair and sat by me. He reached out his hand towards mine and I hesitated for a moment, before taking it. 'Do you not think that if I knew of any other living relatives of yours I would have told you? Do you think I would have left you living out the life of a servant if you had kin to provide for you?'

I did not pull my hand away, but I faced him. 'If it served your interests - I mean the national interests not your personal interests, I grant you that much - to keep me in Richard Stapleford's house then, yes, I think you might have left me there.'

Fitzroy gave a sad little smile. 'Perhaps for a while. Certainly not for ever. I hope we can agree on that.'

'So, my father's siblings do not live?'

'He had one brother and one sister. The brother joined the Royal Navy and was lost at sea before he turned twenty-one. Their sister married but died in childbirth and the baby with her. I am deeply sorry this tale does not have a happier ending. But you have Bertram now. You and he will have a good life. Even your mother has found a new spouse! There is no point in dwelling on the tragedies of the past.'

'I assume you are not going to take credit for The Bishop?' I said wryly.

'Certainly not. No offence, Euphemia, but I intend to

165

stay as far away from your mother as possible.'

I smiled with genuine amusement. 'You are not the only person to feel like that.' Fitzroy smiled back, but it was without his usual mocking undertone. There was an air of sadness about him I didn't understand, and yet I felt it palpably. 'My grandparents, who were they?'

'Mary and John Martins - and believe me, if I was making this up, I would use more exotic names.' His sadness shifted quickly into his usual more sardonic tone. 'She was the daughter of a country squire and he worked as a professor in a boy's school, teaching Latin, Greek, and the classics. Probably where your father got his love of those.'

'How long have you known all this?' I asked.

'I thoroughly research anyone I intend to trust with the affairs of the nation and matters of the crown,' said Fitzroy. 'I cannot afford any of my assets to become compromised. You will understand that.'

'Do you take as much interest in your other assets as you do in me?' I asked boldly.

Fitzroy let go of my hand. 'You are the youngest female asset I have ever employed. I admit, I do feel a certain duty of protection. It is uncomfortable. But I am still in the process of convincing my superiors that the use of females in our trade is an advantage. Also, your maternal grandfather is a person of significance.' He stood up, and against all etiquette, stretched. 'Besides,' he said, 'as I have told you before, you show a remarkable talent for this kind of work.'

I sat up gingerly and took the flannel from my forehead. 'I should find my mother and Bertram. Do you still need me?'

Fitzroy opened his mouth and then closed it again.

Then he said, 'I almost said something most regrettable there.' He gave me a tight little smile. 'Don't you want to be in at the kill?'

'I have never been into blood sports,' I said coldly.

'Let me put it another way. Would you prefer to sit in the coffee lounge with your family for as long as it takes me to wind up this situation, or would you prefer to be active and help me close the case more quickly?'

'The latter,' I said without hesitation.

'Good girl. I think you should visit your mother briefly. It would be most odd of you not to -'

'Obviously.'

'But what I want you to concentrate on is where the manuscript might be hidden. Reading over your notes I believe we are close, but we are still missing vital information. The easiest way to answer many of these questions is to read the document in question.'

'I thought you had people looking?' I said, rising shakily to my feet. Fitzroy was beside me in a moment, his hand under my elbow.

'They are still looking but, so far, to no avail. I think our murderer had a plan and it was liable to have been a neat one, given his training. Helios was one of the best, by all accounts -'

I broke in, 'Did he close the Treaty of Berlin?' I asked.

'No, I didn't get to that bit, did I? We believed one of the team was turned by the Russians. At least that is what Helios told us when Phlegon showed up dead. Now, of course, we believe Phlegon was killed by Helios. But at the time we only knew the team was compromised. All of them were pulled back from Berlin. The civilian assets were released from any further duties and provided with - I admit - weak cover identities. They kept their original names but were found positions in different parts of the country from where they had been recruited. No one expected anyone to go looking for them. It was more a courtesy to give them a chance to start again than what might have been considered protection. But Helios was given a very deep cover. There is no one left alive to my knowledge who knows what was set up for Helios, but such was his reputation at the time the department felt they owed him an entirely new life. No one suspected he was the traitor.'

'But they suspected the other civilians?' I asked.

'I cannot, in all honesty, tell you. You must remember, it was still a long time before I would join the service, and what I am telling you is either hearsay or from the sketchy notes kept at the time. The department was not exactly into paperwork in the early days,' he said with a short laugh. 'It was all a bit derring-do.'

'It seems the department was also much less careful of its civilian assets too.'

'Be fair, Euphemia. Helios was a star - hence his code name. They all thought the sun shone out of his...' He coughed and winked at me. 'You get the idea. That he might be working against the interests of the nation did not occur to anyone for a long time.'

'Who did spot it?' I asked.

'I did, when I inherited the files many years later. Of course, I wasn't quick enough, and all the assets died.'

'Do you blame yourself?'

A mask of detachment spread over the spy's face. Then he flashed me his most charming smile. 'Not as much as I blame Helios.'

'Do you want revenge?'

Fitzroy nodded. 'Revenge for them, and justice for the

worst kind of traitor.'

'I think I am actually flattered that you let me work on this investigation,' I said. 'This means a lot to you.'

Fitzroy stepped away from me. 'More than you know,' he said and held open the door for me. 'And, Euphemia, when you find the manuscript, don't read it. It's imperative you bring it straight to me.' As I passed through the door, he said quietly, 'I am trusting you.'

Chapter Eighteen
An Old Truth Comes to Light

I had the uncanny feeling that Fitzroy had been on the verge of telling me something else. It often felt like he was keeping something back from Bertram and me, because he usually was. However, this was different. He seemed genuinely disturbed by the situation. When he said he was trusting me, I heard an undercurrent of urgency I had never heard before.

Did he fear that as he played Helios at this game of cat and mouse at the Holby, the former master spy might not only outwit him, but do something terrible? Was Helios much more of a danger than he was willing to let us know? I had a strong desire to run to Bertram's side, but whether that was to protect him, or for him to protect me, I was not entirely sure.

I found my mother seated in the coffee lounge with an entourage worthy of an Empress fussing around her. The Bishop, towering over the rest of them, contented himself with keeping his large hand on his wife's shoulder. Richenda was sitting next to her, ineffectively fanning her with a napkin, and Bertram stood alongside clutching a decanter of brandy in his hand. My mother was already sipping from a glass of the stuff. Joe sat a little off to one side, wide-eyed and clearly frightened. I went over and hugged him.

'Mama fainted,' he said. 'Mama never faints. Not even when Papa died.'

'Mama saw an old picture of Papa when he was young.

She didn't know he used to be a member here.' I squeezed him. 'Is that not amazing? We are sitting in a coffee lounge that Papa used when he was young.'

Joe looked around uncertainly. 'Do you really think so?'

'Well, he never smoked, so I imagine he spent much of his time in here, or in the reading room. He did enjoy a good cup of coffee.'

'Ellie made it so badly it used to make him so upset, but he never told her off, because he knew she was doing her best.'[18]

'I had almost forgotten about her,' I said. 'Poor Ellie, she never was very good in the kitchen. I hope she found some nice farmer to marry and didn't have to remain in service. It didn't suit her.'

'It was very like Papa not to scold, wasn't it?' said Joe. 'Step-pa doesn't get cross either. He's got a scary frown, but he is ever so nice. Even if he does talk a lot.' Joe looked up at me. 'Do you think Papa would mind that I like him?' Joe's eyes were full of guilt.

'I think he would be delighted that both you and Mama have found someone who will take good care of you.'

'And you,' said Joe. 'You'll come home now, won't you?'

'I'm going to marry Mr Stapleford.'

Joe watched Bertram hovering ineffectively with the decanter and said, with all the casual cruelty of a child, 'Are you sure?'

'Quite sure,' I said. 'I had better go and talk to Mama. Why don't I get Bertram to come over and say hello? He

---

[18]Ellie was our maid at the vicarage.

could tell you about his motor car. It goes ever so fast.'

Joe's face switched in a flash from dubious approbation to genuine enthusiasm. 'Rather,' he said.

I went over to Bertram and took the decanter from him. He turned to me in surprise. 'I do not think my mother will need more than one,' I said, placing it on a nearby table. 'Thank you for seeing to her. Do you think you could possibly show Joe your motor car? I know we have a lot going on, but he is still a child, and I think today is somewhat overwhelming for him. I take it you can let yourself out of the building?'

'Of course,' said Bertram, relief flooding his face. 'I'd love to.' I watched as he hurried off to suggest this excursion to my little brother, thinking that it would be good for both of them to get away from the Club for a while. I very much wished I could go with them.

'Mama,' I said. 'I am so sorry you had such a dreadful shock. No one seems to have been aware Papa was once a member.'

My mother took a delicate but large sip of brandy. I reflected that she could be the only person I had ever known capable of guzzling brandy with a certain elegance. Richenda carried on flapping the napkin. She did not appear to notice she was wafting crumbs onto my mother. I glanced up at The Bishop, who was calmly surveying the scene below, like a seagull on a cliff. My mother's unoccupied hand crept up and touched The Bishop's lightly. 'I agree, it was a surprise, like opening a window into the past. But I do not wish you to think it was an disagreeable one, Euphemia. I was greatly fond of your father, despite what may have appeared to have been some difficulties while you were growing up.' My mother's cheeks became faintly pinker. I decided to ascribe this to the brandy.

'If The Bishop will excuse my saying so, I have always thought your marriage with Papa a most romantic one,' I said truthfully.[19]

'Have no worries on my account,' said The Bishop, his deep voice booming down from above. 'There are no secrets between your mother and me. We are a most unconventionally close couple.'

'Husband, honestly,' muttered my mother, turning from pink to rose madder.

'I am afraid I never knew your father, Euphemia,' continued The Bishop, 'But I only ever heard him well spoken of in ecclesiastical circles.'

I must have looked surprised, for he continued to reassure me on this at some length. Eventually I had to interrupt. 'I am sorry for my expression. It is simply that my father was barely in the ground before we were called on to vacate the vicarage. If he had been held in such esteem why were his family so treated, and why was he never offered advancement? I know from personal experience he was a great scholar.'

'Euphemia,' said my mother. 'It is not your right to question.'

However, The Bishop gave a broad grin. This made him look more like a giant bird than ever. 'Forgive me,' he said, 'but my acquaintance with your mother began when she assailed me with the very same questions. It was that first encounter that led onto our happy union.'

'I beg your pardon,' I said. 'My mother is right. It is

---

[19]A romantic elopement that ended in much regret, was the whole truth of what I thought.

none of my business.' I cast a side glance at Richenda and raised my eyebrow. Unfortunately, she misinterpreted my message and only flapped the napkin all the faster with worse effect.

'No, not at all,' said The Bishop. 'I understand your curiosity. I looked into the matter for your mother. You will understand I was not involved with that parish at the time. I discovered that your father had been offered advancement on no less than four separate occasions - quite remarkable! - and had turned them all down.'

'Oh, Josiah,' muttered my mother in an undertone of lament.

'He was not only a Classics scholar, as you know, but apparently a polyglot too. Excluding the dead languages, he spoke more than six others with a degree of great fluency. Perhaps you share his talent?'

'I had no idea,' I said. 'He never taught me anything other than Greek and Latin.'

'In which she excelled,' said my mother in a low voice that clearly did not praise my success.

'As to why you were asked to remove so quickly from the vicarage, I read more than one letter of protest about this. Apparently, the request came from outside the Church, but I cannot track down from whom. I only know that the bishop of that diocese felt it was not someone he could refuse. Sadly, he has since died, so I cannot ask him.'

'Obviously, it was your grandfather,' said my mother. 'He has been relentlessly cruel and vindictive since the first day of my marriage to Josiah.'

The Bishop patted her shoulder. 'We will pray for graciousness to enter his soul,' he said.

My mother snorted. She then quickly pretended it was the brandy. As The Bishop bent over her to assure himself she was well, I beckoned to Richenda. She rose quickly and followed me as I left the room.

'Thank goodness for that,' said Richenda. 'My wrists are positively aching. It seems you and your mother are more alike that you knew.'

'What do you mean?' I demanded.

'You're both fainters. I would never have thought it of either of you!'

'These are extreme circumstances,' I said firmly. 'Now, Mr Fitzroy...'

'Oh, that nice policeman,' said Richenda. 'He's rather handsome, isn't he? When he swept you up in his arms, it was -'

'Never mind that,' I said sharply. 'He wants us to find the missing manuscript. He has had people rummaging all over the place, but they have not found a thing. Apparently, he believes we can find it.' I added this to appeal to her vanity. It did not fail.

'I expect he's using men,' said Richenda disparagingly. 'They will all think alike. But then I suppose it was hidden by a man.'

'I cannot tell you much,' I said, 'but the man who hid it - I might as well tell you his codename rather than talking about this man and that - was Helios.'

'How pretty. Like the sun.'

'Exactly. Helios is not your average man.' I took a deep breath and looked up and down the corridor. There was no one in sight. In for a penny, in for a pound. 'In fact, he used to be a spy until he turned traitor. We think Mr Lovelock's memoirs would have exposed the truth about him.'

'No wonder he is wanted by the police,' said Richenda in what I can only describe as accents of delight. 'What a lark!'

'So, you see, he would have had a plan to hide the manuscript and get it safely away from the club. A good plan.'

Richenda nodded eagerly. 'But then you and Bertie came along and managed to mess it all up. How bally unlucky for the chap.'

'Richenda, need I remind you he's a traitor and a murderer!'

'I know. I know. I'm trying to get into his head. If you think about it, he must have been jolly annoyed when he found out about the papers. There he was, happily pootling along, and then he hears about this chappie who is going to expose his deepest, darkest secrets after he's been keeping his nose clean for years. I mean if he had carried on being a traitor someone would have caught up with him before now, would they not?'

I blinked. It was all too easy to forget that underneath her country exterior Richenda could be, when she chose, as sharp as a tack.

'Makes you think, though,' she added. 'Wonder what stopped him being a traitor? I mean, I presume you don't try and sell out your country unless you're getting something from it. Money? Titles? Land?'

I put my finger to my lips. 'You are getting loud and I do not wish to alert him to our activities.'

'Of course, he is still in the building!' exclaimed Richenda, lowering her voice. 'Gosh. Intense. Reminds me of something Amy does.'

'What?' I said with little hope.

'Well, sometimes when she thinks one of us is not

paying her enough attention she'll take something she knows we need. Like Hans' fountain pen when he is meant to be writing, or my hairpins, if she doesn't want me to go out without her. But the thing is, she does not simply hide them, she moves them. She will put them in one place and hope we will search elsewhere. Then when we've searched an area she will move the pen, or whatever, into the area we've already searched. She is such a little sneak. Do you know I once found Hans' best Montblanc planted among the tulips?'

Richenda's smile suggested that she found these escapades endearing. I was about to dismiss her motherly ramblings, when two things struck me. I had a clear mental picture of Hans' favourite green fountain pen planted among the green stems of the tulips. It would be in both plain sight and hidden. Clever Amy! Also, it was more than likely Fitzroy's men were doing a methodical search through the building. Cat and mouse. Neither Bertram nor I had attempted to contain our suspects and Fitzroy must have given it up as a bad job. Helios could be moving with impunity and it would not be difficult for him to move papers from one area to another. Why, all he needed to do was slip them inside a newspaper or book. I grabbed Richenda's shoulders and kissed her forcefully on the forehead. 'You are brilliant,' I said.

'I am!'

'Yes, he is obviously doing what Amy did and moving the papers around ahead or behind the search. No one would think anything of a man with a newspaper – and it would be easy to tuck them inside.'

'There must be a lot of places to hide papers in a Gentlemen's Club,' said Richenda. 'There are even cubbyholes for each member behind the desk.'

'That seems a little too obvious,' I said. 'But it is somewhere to start.'

We returned to Evans' front desk, where we found the man with his top buttonhole undone drinking a cup of tea. He shot to his feet when he saw us and tried to stow the tea quickly out of sight. We all heard the sound of a mug falling over, then rolling off the edge to smash on the ground behind the desk. Evans' expression said it all.

'Can I help you, ladies?' he said in most weary voice.

'We need to look in all the members' partridge holders!' said Richenda excitedly.

'She means pigeonholes,' I corrected.

'You can't do that,' said Evans, aghast.

'We are on the business of the Crown and we can do whatever we want,' said Richenda. 'Do you wish me to fetch some of the men to explain this to you?'

I glanced at her in alarm. However, it had the desired effect on Evans. 'I give up,' he said, throwing up his hands. 'No one ever told me there would be days like this working here. I'll be in my cubby if I'm needed.' He retreated into the back room where the ledgers had been kept. We heard the sound of a bolt being thrown.

'You know we cannot really do whatever we want,' I said to Richenda.

'Poo!' said my soon to be sister-in-law. 'He doesn't know that.' She flipped up the desk top with a little difficulty and went through to the pigeonholes. She began to pull things out.

'Hold on,' I said. 'We must do this properly. We don't want to find something incriminating and then not remember which pigeonhole it came from.'

Richenda sighed. 'Sometimes you are no fun,' she said. But she joined me in going through the items present in careful sequence. We found the usual number of letters sent directly to the club. 'Bills their wives don't know about or love letters from mistresses,' said Richenda. 'We should open them.'

'We have no authority to do so,' I reminded her. I ignored the face she pulled at me and went back to the task. It seemed that the Reverend W. Goodie liked to keep socks in his pigeonhole; fortunately they were clean, if overly darned. We also unearthed a number of newspapers, but despite our initial excitement, when they were unfolded they proved to be no more than they purported to be. Although we did see that Mr F. Richards tended to mark a lot of horses on the racing pages. There were also tickets for the club's Christmas Ball, already purchased. Tickets for concerts and theatre plays, which again made Richenda comment about these obviously not being for legitimate family. She also added it was about time she paid a visit to Hans' club. However, a few worried questions on my part proved that Hans, ever sensible, had never told her which one he belonged to. I thought this wise as, between the death of his first wife and marrying Richenda, we both knew he had had a number of mistresses - and, well, it is not for me to comment further.

A number of the gentlemen also kept mints, boiled sweets, and even cigarettes in the pigeon holes. I could only presume they handed them in so they didn't have to share with other members. A few had left their shoes and were likely wearing slippers, which I thought rather a good idea. Some of the clergymen had left small books of prayers and even religious chains stowed here. Richenda held up one cross admiringly. 'It's very pretty, but I expect it would easily dangle in your soup. The chain is rather long.'

The most intriguing thing we found in an unmarked pigeonhole, was a posy of dried roses and violets.

'I wonder which pigeonhole belonged to your father,' said Richenda.

'Who is to say he even had one,' I said. 'There are certainly fewer spaces than there are members. Perhaps it is a privilege for older members.' But I couldn't help tracing my finger along the edge of the wooden racks, wondering if they had ever held mementoes that my father too had held.

'Well, Wilkes, Prendergast, and Davenport don't appear to have one,' said Richenda.

I checked the list I had complied as we went through. 'Cole-Sutton has several packets of boiled sweets…'

'Liquorice and lemon,' said Richenda. 'What? I was being thorough!'

'They could have been poisoned,' I said. 'This isn't a game, Richenda. In this building is a person who has killed and is likely to kill again. He knows we are seeking him. He isn't going to let us find him easily and he will have no compunction in killing us if we get too close.'

'But we are nothing to him!' said Richenda, paling.

'We are a threat,' I said.

Richenda sat down. 'I am not sure I wish to continue in this.'

'Chapelford,' I continued, 'had half a packet of cigarettes and two silk handkerchiefs. Lovelock had several bottles of ink.'

'How would I know if I had been poisoned?' said Richenda.

'I'd think you'd know by now,' I said as I put back the last items.

'That's comforting,' said Richenda in a worried voice.

'Right, where shall we try next,' I said.

'I meant it. I should stop this,' said Richenda. 'I have children. They need me.'

I bit my tongue before I could suggest she should have thought of this earlier. Preferably before she had forced her way into Bertram's motor car. 'The best action you can take is to help me conclude this affair quickly. The longer it takes, the more danger we are all in. Simply withdrawing from the investigation won't take you off the killer's list. In fact, he might think you had found something.'

'How do you do this?' said Richenda. 'I know this is not your first time involved in an investigation.'

I thought for a moment. 'At first, I did not have much of a choice, but I suppose as time has gone on I have become accustomed to this work. It is rewarding.'

'I am glad to hear you say so,' said a male voice behind me. I turned to see Fitzroy. I felt a very male urge to swear, but I did my best to smile sweetly. He gave me a wry grin, easily reading my thoughts. 'Did you have any luck, ladies?'

'I thought you would want a list,' I said, passing him the paper. 'I can't see anything that sheds any light on the matter, but you may well see something I have missed.'

Fitzroy ran his eye down the paper and shook his head. 'No, I don't.'

'The sweets are only sweets,' I said. 'Richenda ate two...'

Fitzroy raised an eyebrow and finished for me, 'And isn't dead yet?' He turned to the woeful Richenda. 'That was unwise,' he said. 'But I seriously doubt Cole-Sutton's confectionery was poisoned. I expect you will live.'

Richenda gave a little mournful sniff. I saw the edges

of the spy's lips twitch and had to bite my own lip not to laugh out loud. Our eyes met, and I felt the heat come into my face. I understood Fitzroy all too well.

'Well then, carry on,' said the spy, and walked past the policeman straight out the front door.

'Has he gone home?' asked Richenda.

'I never bother asking where he is going,' I said, trying to hide my face from her.

'I suppose a policeman would never answer to a civilian.'

'Hmm,' I said.

'Why, Euphemia! Your face is scarlet.' Her puzzled eyes searched my face and then she glanced over to the door. 'Are you fond of that policeman?' she asked astonished.

'Of course not,' I said.

Richenda did not look convinced. 'Where is Bertram?'

'He's showing my brother his motor car. We should try the reading room next.'

'I think I will come with you after all,' said Richenda. 'I don't want you getting into any trouble.'

I ignored the implication. We methodically searched through the newspapers left on the reading stands and the ones still on the poles. Neither of us spoke. There was only the rustling of paper and the crackling of the small fire in the hearth. Apart from us, the room was empty and showed no sign of recent occupation. As we searched, my mind wandered between trying to put together the small pieces of information I had gathered and the awkward admission that, more often than not, I felt comfortable in Fitzroy's company. Something that, only a year ago, I would have never thought possible. Bertram was right, we needed to separate our lives from the spy if we were ever to have a normal relationship. Fitzroy interfered too often in both our lives - and my private thoughts.

'Have you found anything?' Richenda said. 'You've got the oddest expression on your face.'

I put back the last paper. 'I have found nothing here either. I do like your idea of him moving things around, but I fear our culprit continues to be well ahead of us. I think it is time we braved the smoking room. If nothing else, I can convince the members to leave us to our search by opening the window. I thought they would die of apoplexy last time I opened the sash.'

'Gentlemen do seem to enjoy the smell of smoke. I find it repulsive, but you've joined Bertram in our smoking room before. I did not think you minded it.'

'This is nothing like that,' I said opening the door. 'There is a positive fug in here.'

'You mean people might notice someone going in and out, but they couldn't necessarily say who it was?' said Richenda. 'When did Lovelock die?'

'Somewhere between when he took the key for the room, ten o'clock I believe, being his usual time, and when they tried to deliver his luncheon.'

'You should double-check the time he took the key out,' said Richenda. 'It might give you a smaller window of opportunity. Unless the doctor can be more precise.'

'I don't think a doctor has been called. Bertram was asked to leave that until Fit - until the policeman arrived.'

'I've heard you call him Fitzroy before,' said Richenda. 'I don't see how his name could be a secret.'

We walked along the corridor towards the smoking room. 'There are so many pieces of this puzzle. I keep thinking that I can make them fit, but it is like trying to do a jigsaw where every time you get close to completing it, someone knocks the table over and you have to start all over again. I am certain there is something I am missing. If I could get that one piece…'

'You could steady your table,' said Richenda. 'You do say the oddest things.'

We stormed the bastion of the smoking room, side by side. Wilkes, Prendergast, and Cole-Sutton were still there. None of them looked pleased to see us. Wordlessly I went over to the window and opened it. Prendergast immediately extinguished his cigarette and left. I walked over to the fire and peered down into it. Fitzroy was right, it was smokier than usual. Not by much, by this point, but it may have been worse earlier. Out of the corner of my eye I saw Richenda begin to search among the few books and between the chess sets. Cole-Sutton stood to help her reach the tallest shelves, his cheery voice teasing her about not getting dust on her pretty red hair. Wilkes appeared to be watching them with some amusement. I looked perfunctorily through the papers kept beside the kindling. As I expected, there was nothing out of the ordinary there. It would have been dangerous to leave anything there as much in fear of it being burnt as discovered. I stood up and took stock of the room. Wilkes was now attempting to write in a notebook on his lap. Ash from his cigar trembled dangerously over his scribblings. I had a sudden mental image of the writing desks on the edge of the lobby, where a member could dash out a note or a telegram and hand it to the porter to have it delivered.

As calmly as I could I got up and walked out. Richenda was playfully scolding Cole-Sutton. Neither of them noticed me close the door softly behind me. Wilkes appeared engrossed in writing his note. I found Evans back at the front desk looking less ruffled. At least he was

184

enough in command of himself to offer me a token nod. I nodded back and made my way over to the first of the writing desks.

It was more of a large writing slope. At the top was a niche for a bottle of ink. Small sheets of writing paper with the club's address and motif at the top were clipped on one side. There were also envelopes, a storage space for pens, and a large blotting pad to write on. A member would write his message and then turn it over and press it against the pad to stop the ink smudging. When the blotting page had become too covered it was simply removed to reveal a fresh sheet underneath. With my fingers trembling I reached under the first two sheets of the blotting paper and encountered the rough edges of something. Doing my best to keep out of the eye-line of Evans I searched the desks one by one. My excitement grew as under each blotting pad I found sheets of written paper. There were also more stuffed between each desk and the wall. At the last desk, which was nearest to the door, I attempted to assemble my find. It was a surprising number of pages.

The writing was small, cramped, and frequently scored through and overwritten. I could not positively say I had found the missing papers until I got them into some kind of order. I recalled Fitzroy's entreaty for me not to read them and I had no intention of ruining my eyesight by trying. Fortunately, Lovelock had written with page numbers. At last I came to the title page. This was written in a much clearer script. It read 'An account of the desperate events behind the Treaty of Berlin, taking place on the date of June 10th 1878.'

So, we had been right, this was about the first team who had been sent out to Berlin. Could Lovelock have known Helios' true name? Despite my promise, I could not help turning to the first page. I would only scan the opening paragraphs, I told myself. I would tell no one. My eye ran down the page. The script was difficult and the grammar tediously correct. The wording was overblown and grandiose. It was the fifth paragraph at the bottom of the page where I found the phrase 'the intelligence person accompanying the envoy was known only as Helios. A bombastic individual, overly aware of his own worth. I and the others underrated both his ruthlessness and his skill. Josiah Martins, our linguist, stated from the beginning that he found being in the man's company uncomfortable. He was the only one to express doubts over this star of the new intelligence department that had so recently begun operation. Josiah, who was my good friend since we met at college, saw deeper into the souls of others than many...'

I forced myself to break off reading. I found myself clinging to the front of the desk. My legs quivered beneath me, but I was determined not to faint. Could this be true, that my father had formed part of that delegation? My mind refused to grasp the implications. Did this mean my father had been one of the civilian assets? Not Phlegon, obviously, but one of the others? Could it be that he had spent his life hiding from his past? Was this why he had always refused promotion? Had he tried to live a quiet country life to protect us - myself, my mother, and little Joe? Did my mother know? I felt certain she did not. She had hated my father's lowly position. She recognised his genius and could never understand why he was content with such a limited lifestyle. It had driven a wedge between them. But was it all to protect us? Did he fear the past reaching out to claim him?

I leaned heavily against the desk. Dear God, had he been murdered? Had Helios claimed him? I had to find

Fitzroy. I had to tell him... I took a step and stopped. It felt like a thunder clap went off in my head. He knew! Of course, he knew! How hard had he tried to sideline me in this investigation? How kind had he been to me? Almost affectionate in his attempts to distract me. The lies. He had always lied, but these lies were damnable. Not telling me that my father was a member of the club so as not to distress me. He had manipulated me at every turn. Oh God! Oh God! He said he felt he had failed the assets. Fitzroy was responsible for my father's death. He hadn't been interested in an old case until he realised people were dying, and even then he had not been quick enough. I knew him well enough to know he was unusually intelligent. If he had truly focused his attention on this case I felt sure he could have saved my father. But it had not been of enough interest to him to prioritise.

I dashed bitter tears from my cheeks. He had let Helios slip right past him and continue killing. My tears were flowing freely now. He did not want me to know because he knew I would - I would what? Hate him? That much was certain. Or was it simply that he didn't want to lose an asset? My father had trained me in many unusual ways for a girl. Had he inadvertently made me of interest to Fitzroy because my skills were useful to him? The service had used my father and then Fitzroy, in turn, had used me. Everything. Everything from the very beginning had been a lie. Eric - Lord Milton to give him his true name - had controlled me at every turn. I had been foolish, weak and unbearably gullible. Bertram had been right all along, Fitzroy was not only dangerous, he was immoral and cared for nothing but his allegiance to the crown.

The door to the club opened. I turned away. The doorman spoke. 'Certainly, sir.'

I heard the footsteps stop behind me.

'Euphemia,' said Fitzroy. 'Are you all right?'

I turned to face him. Then I slapped him as hard as I could.

Fitzroy didn't flinch. 'Your father was Aethon. I warned him, really I did, but he didn't listen.'

I went to slap him again.

Chapter Nineteen
Fitzroy Admits to The Unforgivable

Fitzroy caught my wrist and held it tightly. 'How much did you read?' he asked calmly.

'The opening page,' I said. 'Do not worry, I do not know any more of your grubby little secrets.'

'Where is it?'

'Let me go and I'll give it to you.'

Fitzroy released me, but took a cautionary step back so I could not strike him again. I thrust the papers at him. 'Here is your precious manuscript. It is too short to be finished, and I doubt what there is of it names Helios.'

'Not on the first page at least,' said Fitzroy, without taking them.

I pushed the papers at him again. This time he took them. 'I told you not to read it,' he said. 'I knew this would only distress you.'

'Please, do not try to convince me you are concerned for my state of mind,' I sobbed. Angrily I brushed away tears from my face. I hated that I could not stop crying. 'You have done nothing but deceive me from the first.'

'You are very wrong,' said Fitzroy, his voice low, 'I have done nothing but try to protect you. I brought you into the service so I could keep you under my watchful eye after your father died. That you have proved so effective has been an unforeseen bonus. I have done everything I could to keep you safe and to help you become well-established.'

'Do not even dare to take credit for Bertram loving

me!' I said. 'Do not even dare. He is a far better man than you will ever be.'

'On that we can agree,' said the spy softly.

I felt a wave of emotion building up inside me. I wanted to shout and rage at him, but I had still enough sense to know I did not want to draw the killer's attention to the finding of the papers.

'You are upset,' said Fitzroy. 'That is understandable.'

I had to bite the inside of my mouth not to scream at him. It hurt. I tasted blood. Fitzroy continued to speak in a low, soft voice, but I did not listen to a single word. I pushed past him and fled. No footsteps followed me.

I ran into the coffee room and, sighting my mother beside The Bishop, did something I had not done since I was six years old. I flung myself into her arms, weeping.

My mother felt stiff against me, but within moments her arms came tightly around me. 'Who has had the audacity to distress my daughter?' she said in voice that boded ill for even Fitzroy.

'Perhaps we should remove ourselves to another room,' said The Bishop. I was still sobbing violently. 'I believe Euphemia might require some time to recover. Ah, here is Bertram. Bring the brandy along, will you, there's a good chap. Joe, you had better come too.'

I believe I came as close to real hysteria that day than at any other time in my life to date. I was only vaguely aware of being helped from the room. The Bishop procured a key from the front desk and took all of us into one of the smaller private chambers – although, thankfully, not the one in which Lovelock had been found. It had a similarly sized desk but was slightly larger than Lovelock's room. Chairs were provided for my mother and myself. As I gradually pulled myself together I was aware Bertram, The Bishop, and Joe were standing around in various states of awkwardness. My mother held the brandy glass. From time to time she made me take a sip. Once the initial emotional storm was over, she fell back into what I knew as her usual persona. 'Honestly, Euphemia, what a scene you made! I hope you had good reason.'

'I rather hope she didn't!' said Bertram stoutly.

'Ah, yes, quite,' said The Bishop. 'From what you have told me of Euphemia's character, this display is much at odds with her normal demeanour.'

'Are you hurt?' demanded my mother. She looked me over as if she were checking the seams on a dress. 'I cannot see any sign of injury,' she said.

'Fitzroy,' I said, hiccupping as I swallowed my last tears.

Bertram uttered a cry of rage. 'What has the bounder done?' he demanded.

'That name,' said my mother, 'it seems vaguely familiar. Do we know any Fitzroys, Husband?'

'He is the Crown Agent we have been working for,' I said.

Little Joe let out an 'oh' of surprise. 'Are you a spy, Euphemia?'

'No,' I said. 'But Bertram and I have both had the misfortune of being called upon by the British Secret Service to aid them.'

'Euphemia, I will not listen to fairy tales,' said my mother.

'She is quite correct, ma'am,' said Bertram. 'It is not anything either of us wanted to be involved with, but when called upon to do one's duty for King and Country, one has to answer.'

'Of course,' said The Bishop. 'But it is unusual, is it not, to involve a young woman?'

'That is what I have always thought,' said Bertram. 'But apparently Euphemia is particularly gifted at this sort of work. At least according to Fitzroy.' Then he obviously remembered where the conversation had started. 'What did the cad do?'

I dried my tears with the last scrap of dry cloth on my very wet handkerchief. I looked around the room. 'I do not know if I am allowed to say.'

'Dammit,' said Bertram. 'You can tell me. We are under the same oath.'

'But I am unsure of everyone else.'

'That is ridiculous,' said my mother.

'Actually, it's not,' said Bertram, contradicting my mother for the second time without fear. 'There are severe penalties for betraying state secrets.'

'I am her mother! I demand to know.'

'So, it's a secret,' said Bertram, 'that has you so upset. Fitzroy didn't actually do anything?'

I looked at him puzzled.

'I mean nothing…physical,' said Bertram blushing a crimson red. 'He didn't try to kiss you or anything?'

'Good God, no!' I said and earned myself a reproving look from The Bishop. 'If anything, it was the other way round.'

'You kissed him!' said Bertram and Joe together in varying degrees of horror.

'Of course not,' I said. 'I slapped him.'

'Oh well, that's all right,' said Bertram. 'If you ask me, that man has been asking for a damn good slap for a long time.' He addressed my mother and stepfather, 'He is insufferably smug and secretive. Only just scrapes by as a gentleman. Probably dragged up in a gutter somewhere.'

'He's a Lord,' I said. 'Minor title,' I added for my mother's benefit. 'I doubt it's hereditary.'

'No one worth worrying over, then,' said my mother. This time The Bishop gave her a reproving look.

'Why did he make you cry, Effie?' asked Joe plaintively, falling back on his childish nickname for me.[20]

I shrugged helplessly. 'I really don't think I can tell you.' Tears trickled down the side of my nose. 'It is so unfair!' I exclaimed.

It was at this point that Fitzroy stepped into the room. He acknowledged everyone with a nod. 'How much has Euphemia told you?' he asked, coming right to the point.

I wouldn't even look at him, so it was left to Bertram to answer, 'Nothing, except that she slapped you because she learned something that distressed her.'

Fitzroy went over to the desk and sat on it, so everyone in the room swivelled their attention to him. 'Normally, I would deny all knowledge of it, but...' He sighed. 'Need I say that what I will tell you must not be repeated? Not only my life would be forfeit if this episode ever came to light.' His gaze flickered to Joe. 'I repeat, *none of you* must ever mention what I will tell you now.' He gave a wry smile. 'Besides, it would only be denied.'

'I know you,' said my mother. 'You came to the vicarage shortly before my first husband died. You argued with him. I could hear you shouting in our library.'

Fitzroy nodded. 'I thought you might remember me. I came to warn your late husband, Mrs Hawthorn, that his

---

[20]When you are two years old, Euphemia is far too much of a mouthful to bother with.

life was in danger.'

'Are you a doctor?' asked little Joe.

'No, I'm a spy, Joe,' said Fitzroy. 'I came to tell your father than a man, a former agent of the Crown turned traitor, and whom I knew only as Helios, might mean harm to your father. I begged him to tell me if he knew where Helios might be, or even his real name. Your father did not believe a word I said.'

'My husband died of a heart attack,' said my mother. 'You may have brought that closer with your argument, but there was no Helios involved.'

'Oh, but there was. You see, his food was poisoned with digitalis,' said Fitzroy.

'How the devil would you know that?' said The Bishop sharply.

Fitzroy did not comment. It was left to Bertram to say, 'There is only one way, other than being the poisoner himself, that he could know.'

I followed his logic slowly. Then I shot out of my seat. 'You had his body exhumed! That is why you wanted the family away from the vicarage so quickly!'

'Mama?' said little Joe in a small voice. I saw Bertram put an arm around his shoulder and say something softly.

'It is right for a child to hear this?' said The Bishop, his voice now tinged with anger.

'I generally don't have time for niceties,' said Fitzroy. 'That is why I am not a diplomat. I think it better that you all know the truth, although I caution you again, on your honour, not to repeat a word I have said. The whole situation would be completely disavowed, and you might find your lives becoming inexplicably more difficult.'

My mother caught my arm. 'Sit down, Euphemia. I believe we need to hear what this man has to say.' I complied, because I wanted them all to know.

'Josiah Martins was a polyglot. That means, Joe, that he spoke a remarkable number of languages with ease. He accompanied the first British envoy to Berlin in 1878 shortly after he left Cambridge University. However, one of the team died, and it was assumed at the time the dead man was a traitor. The whole team was brought back to England and another sent out to work on the final treaty. The agent who had led the team was given an entirely new identity and life. All his information was expunged from our records. Any mention of him in reports is merely by his codename, Helios. The other civilian assets were given reassignments to a different area of the country, but otherwise their identities and their lives did not change, and they were never asked to work for the Crown again. We feared one or more of them could have been compromised.'

'My Papa was a spy!' said Little Joe with awe.

'He worked with spies,' corrected Fitzroy with a slight smile. 'He was a good and moral man. That alone would disqualify him from being a spy, but he was more than eager to do his duty by Sovereign and Country.'

'But Helios found him,' said my mother. 'How are you involved, Mr Fitzroy? You are clearly too young to have been in Berlin yourself.'

'I inherited the case,' said the spy. 'I was given a watching brief on all remaining civilian assets. I am afraid I was too slow on the uptake. Helios slowly killed them off, one by one. When I finally did realise that something was wrong, I looked back over the case and spoke to as many of the personnel who had been present at the Treaty of Berlin that were left alive. It took a great deal of time and effort and had to be fitted in among my other duties. It was, therefore, only three years ago that I concluded Helios was really the guilty party. This is when I went to warn Mr Martins, the last of the surviving assets.'

'But he did not believe you,' said my mother. 'You cannot have made a compelling case.'

'Perhaps not,' said Fitzroy. 'Your husband had known Helios, and while I eventually got him to admit he had at first had some niggling doubts about the man, he had eventually, like so many others, fallen under this master manipulator's spell. Though I suspect, even if he had felt some qualms about Helios, your husband's own sense of honour could not allow him to even imagine the treachery I was asking him to accept. His refusal cost him his life. After he died I kept an eye on Euphemia. It was known she had been especially close to her father, and it was not inconceivable that Helios might imagine that Josiah had told her about what had happened in Berlin. Killian Lovelock was not part of the official team, so it was quite some time before I unearthed him. But as soon as I did, and I heard about his memoirs, I set a watch on him as well. I knew that Helios could not risk that book ever being published.'

'Did you warn him too?' said my mother.

Fitzroy shook his head. 'He was an old man, without family.'

'May God have mercy on your soul,' said The Bishop.

'Currently Helios is trapped in this building. However, I still do not have an identification. Euphemia and Bertram were working on that for me when Euphemia, unfortunately, discovered her father's role in this tragedy.'

'You never told her,' said Bertram. 'You utter b…'

At this moment, my mother stood up. For a moment I thought she was going to attack the spy. He didn't flinch, but I saw him pale. Instead, my mother put her hands over Joe's ears. 'I may abhor your language, Mr Stapleford,' she said, 'but not your opinion.'

'It is all most wicked and unfortunate,' said The Bishop sadly.

'You must admit, Mother, that it explains a lot about both Father's behaviour and our eviction from the vicarage,' I said.

'I take it Reverend Martins was once again interred with a proper Christian burial,' said The Bishop.

Fitzroy nodded. 'I will attempt to make myself available to answer further questions on another occasion, but now I must turn my attention to the situation in hand. Now, Bertram and Euphemia, I still require your assistance.'

'You cannot possibly ask my daughter to work alongside a man who allowed her father to die through his own inaction?' said my mother coldly.

'I believe your daughter would rather seek justice for her father than bother about my involvement,' said Fitzroy.

My mother began to protest, but I silenced her. 'He is correct, Mother. I wish justice for Papa.' I finally faced the spy. I found his expression completely unreadable. 'However, I have told you everything I discovered. I gave you what I found of the memoirs.'

'And they do not name Helios,' said Fitzroy.

'So, we are back at square one, again,' said Bertram. 'Will this nightmare never end?'

'That is why you decided to speak with my family, is it not?' I said. 'You knew I would never help you if you denied them true understanding of the circumstances of my father's demise.'

'It was the liver that was poisoned, I suppose,' said my mother, caught between anger and tears. 'Such an uncouth dish. None of us would ever touch it, but he did love it so.'

'What made you think of the writing desks?' said Fitzroy.

'It was something Richenda said - where is she, by the way?'

'Stuffing herself with cake, I imagine,' said the spy. 'What did she say?'

'Two things really. It was about her daughter.' Fitzroy gave a sigh of irritation. I ignored him and continued. 'She said when Amy stole things for attention, she would hide them in the most obvious places. Like planting a green pen among tulip stems in a garden.'

'She must be a most ill-disciplined child,' said my mother.

'She is a scamp,' I said.

'All right, I follow the hiding-in-plain sight idea,' said Fitzroy. 'What else?'

'That Amy would move her prize during the day, so that she would put it into rooms Richenda believed had already been searched. In that manner she could keep something hidden for quite some time.'

Fitzroy nodded. 'I see. It is not as helpful as I had hoped. I take it you saw the constables searching the writing desks and decided to try there?'

'No,' I said. 'I haven't come across any of your men.'

'So why there?' said the spy.

'I suppose because of the association with writing,' said Bertram.

'No, that wasn't it. I didn't even remember the desks existed until I - until I saw Wilkes writing a note on his lap.' I looked up into Fitzroy's eyes and saw my understanding reflected in his. Without another word, Fitzroy ran from the room with me hot on his heels.

Chapter Twenty
A Bloody Ending

Fitzroy pelted along the corridor in front of me, but I had been living in the country for some time now and I was fitter than I had been for many years. I caught up to him at the door to the Smoking Room.

'Stand back,' he said softly. 'This will be dangerous.'

'That is why you should not face him alone,' I said equally quietly.

At this point most gentlemen would have insisted a young lady left. Fitzroy did not. He merely nodded. If only he had not... Whatever else, I valued that he respected me as a person and not some frail flower to protect. Behind me I could hear Bertram's heavy steps.

Fitzroy cocked an ear. 'It has to be now,' he said. I knew he meant before Bertram's well-meaning intervention forewarned Helios. 'Ready?'

I nodded, and Fitzroy opened the door.

The window remained open and the air felt cool on our faces. Fitzroy froze on the threshold with me beside him. Between us we completely blocked the doorway. I felt myself tremble, but this was not due to the falling temperature. Before us stood Wilkes, who we now realised was Helios. He had written on his lap rather than risk drawing attention to the writing desks where he had last hidden the memoirs. He stood by the fire, a pleasant smile on his face, and the edge of a knife resting against Richenda's jugular vein. She was white as ash, but neither cried nor struggled. Her eyes were rimmed red, but she appeared to be composed.

'I was wondering how long it would take you to work it out,' said Helios in his well-spoken tones. 'I do not believe you are quite as sharp as your reputation suggests, Fitzroy. It has been altogether disappointing. You seem to rely on women to do your work for you.'

'Your maternal grandmother was Bulgarian, wasn't she? What did the Russians promise you? Land and titles? You must have felt such a fool when you learned they had no intention of supporting your motherland's presence at the Treaty?' said Fitzroy.

'At least you did your homework,' said Wilkes. 'It is a pity it took you so long. You could not save her father, could you? You must have been most upset to learn your dear mentor's mistakes cost your father his life, Miss Martins.'

If Fitzroy had taught me anything he had taught me that when someone goads you, they are desperate for a reaction. They know they are losing. The best action you can take in return is to retain your composure.

'Good afternoon, Richenda,' I said as if nothing was out of the ordinary. 'I should have known you would get to the solution before me. You think most creatively.'

'Thank you,' said Richenda weakly. Her eyes pleaded with me to rescue her. I knew she needed to stay calm. 'Bit of an accident, really.'

'Oh, that's how a great many discoveries are made,' I said cheerily. 'It will all be fine now.'

'Exactly what I was going to say,' said Wilkes. 'I am quite happy to disappear into obscurity once more. You are well aware that is within my skill set. I only ask that my son is allowed to continue in his career without interruption or stain on his reputation.'

'I can guarantee that,' said Fitzroy. 'I've never been a fan of visiting the sins of the fathers on their sons. But, of course, for that to happen, you will have to face justice.'

'Which would expose us both in a way that is unacceptable,' said Wilkes. 'By the way, Euphemia, your father's death was as quick as I could arrange under the circumstances. He was an excellent man, but far too intelligent for his own good. I knew once Fitzroy had visited him he would work things out. A naturally trusting man, Josiah, but not a stupid one by far. Ironic, isn't it, that your companion there signed your father's death warrant when he tried to warn him?'

I felt myself tremble again. At my side Fitzroy briefly pressed his left hand against mine. I felt the crookedness of his broken fingers. I remembered when we had faced death together. He squeezed two of my fingers briefly.

'You appear to have a problem,' I said calmly. 'We are blocking the only exit from the room.'

'I don't think so,' said Wilkes. 'You will not wish harm to come to your future sister-in-law, and Fitzroy so hates innocent life going to waste. It's his biggest flaw.'

Fitzroy pressed my hand as if to urge me forward. I took my cue and stepped slightly into the room, shielding him partly from sight. I had no idea what he intended to do, but for one last time I would trust him.

'Are you sure you have your facts correct? When I first encountered Richenda she abused me quite badly when I worked as a maid in her father's house. She did elevate me to her companion, but only to flaunt her husband in my face. A man I loved, but who she effectively bought. He needed a dowry and I did not have one. I don't know if she got more pleasure out of bedding him in the same house as

I slept in or attempting to show me that money always wins over love. Frankly, if you kill her, you will be doing me a favour.'

Richenda's eyes filled with tears. I could see her biting her lip to hold back the sobs. I wondered if she would ever forgive me.

'So, the apple falls far from the tree,' said Wilkes. 'As a gentleman I deplore your sentiments. As an agent I can only approve of your methods. Fitzroy has had a more complete revenge on Josiah than I could ever have managed. He has cast you in his own image.'

'Euphemia, say it is not true,' pleaded Richenda.

I prayed inwardly that whatever Fitzroy was going to do, he would do it soon. My tactic might have distracted Wilkes, but Richenda was now a dangerous variable in an extremely volatile situation.

'Come now, Richenda. You always knew how Hans and I felt about each other. Even today, you were bitter when you saw us holding hands.'

'What do you say, Fitzroy, give me safe passage out of here and I will release the woman tomorrow.'

'Unharmed?' Fitzroy spoke from behind me.

'Unharmed,' said Wilkes, his expression smug, quite confident that he had won.

'I don't think so,' said Fitzroy. 'You are correct, I do not like to waste an innocent life, but I have become fond of Euphemia. I'd like to see her well established. What I cannot stand is traitors evading justice. In many ways I am considered to be of an immoral nature, but on that I hold firm.' So saying, he brushed gently past me and levelled a gun at Wilkes. I realised that he had used me as cover while he withdrew the firearm from under his jacket. I found that I did not mind. However, I minded very much if

Richenda was to be hurt.

'Come. Come. Do you really think you can fire before…'

Fitzroy fired before Wilkes could even complete his sentence. The bullet pierced his shoulder and, after an incredulous look at his own blood flowing out of the wound, Wilkes staggered backwards, releasing Richenda. I reached out and pulled her clear.

'It was all lies,' I whispered urgently in her ears. 'I had to distract him. Now go.' I pushed her past me and out of danger. I closed the door. It did not occur to me to follow her.

Wilkes sat down heavily in a chair. One hand clenched against his wound. 'I might have hoped that if you were going to risk the woman you would have done it cleanly,' he said. His voice was level but sweat beaded on his face and his breathing was shallow. 'This is only a flesh wound.'

Fitzroy moved further into the room. He kept the gun trained on Wilkes. 'I would have,' said Fitzroy. 'But my damned hands. Got all messed up under torture. I simply can't shoot straight, unless I am close to my target.'

'I see,' said Wilkes. 'Then your offer of justice?'

'There is only one way your son will remain unaffected.'

'Do you give me your word as an agent of the Crown on that? That no action will be taken against him?

'I do,' said Fitzroy.

Wilkes nodded. He closed his eyes. 'Do it,' he said.

Fitzroy didn't turn, but he said, 'You may wish to leave, Euphemia.'

I stepped up beside him. 'No,' I said.

'Then look away,' he insisted. I obeyed, though it felt

cowardly.

Fitzroy fired again and this time, when I looked back, there could be no doubt that Wilkes, also known as Helios, was dead. The man who had killed my father, and so many others, had finally been brought to justice.

Proudly published by Accent Press

www.accentpress.co.uk

Lightning Source UK Ltd.
Milton Keynes UK
UKHW042322270119
336326UK00001B/16/P

9 781786 156488